"You've gone way over your limit on your Western charge card,"

Mrs Myers stated bluntly. "I'm afraid we'll have to cancel your card and set up a repayment schedule."

KC was mortified. At the moment she would have done anything to convince Courtney Conner, who had just overheard the whole humiliating interlude, that she wasn't a loser. She opened her briefcase and fingered the Soccer, Inc. money.

"I'd like to pay the whole thing off. That was my intention all along," KC said. She counted out three hundred and eighty dollars from her Soccer, Inc. fund, ignored the sickening feeling in her stomach, and handed it over to pay off the card.

FRESHMAN LIES

LINDA A. COONEY

Lions
An Imprint of HarperCollinsPublishers

First published in the U.S.A. in 1990 by
HarperPaperbacks
First published in the U.K. in Lions in 1991

Lions is an imprint of
HarperCollins Children's Books,
part of HarperCollins Publishers Ltd,
77-85 Fulham Palace Road
Hammersmith, London W6 8JB

Printed and bound in Great Britain by
HarperCollins Manufacturing Ltd, Glasgow

One

....

He wore a University of Springfield parka that flapped open as he jogged through the spongy rain. He lunged into KC's path, his knit cap tumbling, exposing silky blond hair. Catching the hat as if it were a hard line drive, he looked to KC for appreciation.

"Don't I know you from somewhere?" he asked.

KC had never seen the guy before.

They were heading past the dining commons, which smelled warm and salty. He carried an umbrella and a university-bookstore bag.

KC stared straight ahead and kept on walking.

"Do I know you from Denver?"

"No."

"Summer camp?"

"I doubt it."

"Reform school?"

"Very funny."

"I wouldn't forget a girl who looks like you." He leered. "Where are you going?"

"To meet my girlfriends," she snapped. "Buzz off."

He hurried to keep up with her. "What a coincidence. My name is Buzz."

"Buzz?" KC gave him an icy smile. "Is that a name?"

He whipped out his student ID. "My last name isn't Off, though."

"Too bad."

"What's your name?"

KC wasn't about to admit that her hippie parents had named her Kahia Cayanne.

"Okay, don't tell me. What dorm are you in?"

She didn't tell him she lived alone in an all-girls study dorm, either.

"What's your major?"

KC strode faster.

"You're the quiet type, aren't you?" He stepped up his pace to keep up with her. "I met you last week, during freshman orientation. I'm sure of it."

"I don't think so."

"The toga party?"

"I didn't go."

He looked her up and down, taking in her long, dark curls and her gray eyes, her briefcase, blazer, and knife-pleated skirt. "Oh. I get it. Sorority type. You were rushing with the geeks."

KC flinched. "The Greeks."

"That's what I said. The geeks."

"Ha ha."

"So what sorority house did you get into? And more important, do you still date poor, lonely dorm dudes who think you're gorgeous?" He put a hand to his heart and pretended to grovel.

KC glared.

"Are you reserved for frat brats?"

"I'm not reserved for anyone."

"So what house did you get into?"

KC's rage began to swell.

"Come on."

"Leave me alone!"

"You can tell me. Come on. Which house?"

Suddenly KC spun around and yelled in Buzz's face, "For your information, I'm not in any sorority. I'm a business major and I've never been to Denver, and I'm not interested in dating anybody! *So buzz off, Buzz!*"

"Hey, okay." Buzz backed away. "I just asked. You can't blame a guy for trying." He finally hung back and let her go.

"Guys," KC grumbled, breaking into a run and heading for Faith's dorm.

All KC needed was some guy hassling her about sororities and rush. Guys had caused plenty of trouble the week before for her old friends, Faith Crowley and Winnie Gottlieb. One guy had caused horrible trouble for Faith's roommate, Lauren. And the last thing KC needed was some guy causing trouble for *her*.

"It's KC Angeletti going out for a pass!"

"Winnie, do we have to play this?" KC grumbled.

"Grab it, KC! It's coming right at you," Faith yelled.

"See, Faith agrees. Flip a Frisbee. Classes start tomorrow. This is our last night to goof around without guilt."

It was almost dinnertime. Light was slipping away, and the snap of fall was in the air. KC had let Winnie talk her and Faith into a game of Frisbee on the soggy dorm green. The drizzle had stopped, but there were gooey puddles on the walkways and the grass.

Winnie threw the Frisbee at KC again and resumed her commentary. "Angeletti leaps. She runs. She's going, going . . ."

"Heads up, KC!" Faith cried out.

KC just stood there as the Frisbee drifted back, then

hung in midair. She finally caught it before it dropped onto her head.

Winnie cheered. "Angeletti makes the catch! She fakes a toss to Faith Crowley, who never fakes anything. But Crowley may get penalized for holding. One, two—*bzzz*!" Winnie posed in her purple tights, black minidress, and boots decorated with jingle bells. "Time's up. Do not pass go. Do not think about classes starting and all the homework I'm going to turn in late."

KC tossed the Frisbee to Faith and left the game. She flopped down on a wooden bench and looked off at the dorms that rimmed the green. She saw the old houses, one of which was her dorm, the sterile new dorms, where Winnie lived, and the brick fifties-style complex, where Faith roomed with Lauren Turnbell-Smythe.

Faith called after her, "Come on, KC. Tomorrow even Winnie will have to start going to the library, and I'll be at rehearsal every night. Let's play." She crouched, slapping the Frisbee into her palm.

"I'm not dressed for Frisbee," KC reminded her. She wasn't in the mood for Frisbee, either—not after what had happened during orientation week. Not considering what she was about to face again.

"Okay. I give up." Faith tossed the Frisbee back to Winnie and joined KC. In her denim skirt, cowboy boots, and cable-knit sweater, she wasn't dressed for

Frisbee, either. A satin ribbon was woven through her long braid, and she wore the comedy/tragedy pin she'd won at a high-school drama festival.

"You okay, KC?" Faith soothed, sitting down next to her.

KC shrugged. "I'll be okay. Thanks."

Winnie stuck the Frisbee on her head and jogged over to join her friends. "KC, don't worry."

"I'm not worried," KC bluffed. "I was just thinking about the guy that hassled me today. The one I told you two about. I still can't believe his name was really Buzz."

"I can't believe you wouldn't even tell him your name," Winnie teased. "If it had been me, Buzz and I would have been a serious item by now."

Faith laughed. "And by tomorrow, you and Buzz would no longer be an item, and you'd be having a nervous breakdown."

Winnie grabbed her throat and crumpled onto KC's lap. "The truth hurts."

"Let's forget about guys for tonight at least," Faith begged. She leaned against KC's shoulder. "No more talking about guys, period."

KC nodded. She hadn't admitted why the encounter with Buzz had bugged her so much. She hadn't mentioned that he'd made her think about the sorority she hadn't gotten into, which made her worry about the money she didn't have.

Faith hooked her arm through KC's. "We're counting on you to distract us from guys, KC. You're the tough-minded one of this fearsome threesome. And I don't want to keep thinking about my breakup with Brooks."

"Ditto." Winnie grinned at Faith. "Not that I've ever thought much about breaking up with Brooks. But if I think about Josh too much I may get even crazier than I am already."

"Well, we wouldn't want that." KC had to admire her old friends' humor. Especially after what they'd been through during orientation week. Winnie had thrown herself at Josh, another freshman in her dorm, which had turned out to be a disaster. And Faith had suddenly broken up with Brooks, who'd been her boyfriend since ninth grade.

"You two are amazing," KC said.

"Very true," Winnie agreed.

Faith nodded. "We are amazing humans. No doubt about it."

KC gave them each a hug. Then they sat for a moment watching students tromp across the lawn and head for the dining commons.

"When's Lauren supposed to pick us up?" KC asked.

"Soon." Faith looked off at the dorm parking lot. "I was so relieved when she finally called me today.

I was afraid she was going to leave the university for good after what happened."

"I thought maybe she ran away and joined the circus. That's what I would have done." Winnie snorted. "Actually, I don't blame her for disappearing after that horrible Dream Date Dance."

Thinking about Lauren Turnbell-Smythe and the Dream Date Dance made KC feel sick. She didn't want to remember how rich, lonely Lauren had trusted her, how they had rushed the prestigious Tri Beta sorority together, how Lauren had been set up for a humiliating prank at the dance and KC did nothing to stop it.

Faith soothed, "Don't blame yourself, KC. You did what you could to make up for what happened."

"You did," Winnie seconded.

"I know." KC found some consolation in the fact that she'd finally stood up for Lauren—after the fact. She'd dumped a tray of drinks on a nasty sorority sister named Marielle. That act of revenge had lost KC her chance at joining the sorority. It had also meant getting fired from her waitress job, and without that income, KC's bank account was at zero.

But there was no more time for worries or regrets, because when KC lifted her face again, she saw Lauren no more than ten feet away. Lauren had arrived so quietly that it was almost as if she'd appeared out of thin air. She walked as if she were wounded. Her chubby body looked tired. Her violet eyes had lost their glimmer. Even her normally fluffy beige hair and cashmere coat looked wilted and depressed.

"Hi," Lauren said, glancing from Faith to Winnie and back to Faith again. She avoided looking at KC.

Faith and Winnie jumped up to hug her. KC didn't move.

"We missed you."

"We're really glad you're back."

Lauren gave a half-smile. "Thanks." Her eyes skirted over in KC's direction, but didn't linger. "How are you all?"

"I'm the same," Winnie chattered. "But Faith is going to be the assistant director for *Stop The World, I Want To Get Off.* Isn't that great? How many theater-arts majors would get to do something like that their first semester?"

"We start tomorrow night." Faith looked down. "Some other stuff happened, too, Lauren. With Brooks. I'll tell you about it over dinner."

KC finally stood up. "What about you, Lauren?"

"Me?" Lauren stammered. "I just stayed with my mom at her hotel. I, um, wanted to spend more time with her before she went back home."

"But you can't stand your mom," Winnie blurted.

Faith shushed her.

Lauren began to ramble defensively. "I, um, decided to join the Tri Beta sorority. I really think I'll like it there . . . eventually. It *is* the best sorority on campus. And my mother thinks it's important for my future to be a member. Besides, everyone gets tested during rush.''

"Gross!" Winnie objected. "What they did to you was more than a test.''

Faith took Lauren's arm, leading her toward the parking lot and away from motor-mouthed Winnie. "Lauren, if you want to join the Tri Betas, it's your decision.''

Winnie shook her head and followed.

KC lagged behind. She was beginning to feel as if everything at U of S were stacked against her. The Tri Betas hadn't even wanted Lauren, but they'd asked her to join anyway, because she was rich. And KC, who had the looks and the drive to be real Tri Beta material, was left out in the cold. Even though KC thought some of the Tri Betas were jerks, the injustice of it all made her want to scream.

When KC reached the parking lot, she saw Winnie and Faith admiring Lauren's car. KC tried not to stare at the sparkling white BMW.

"It's really nice of you to take us all to dinner,'' Faith told Lauren as she and Winnie climbed in the backseat. "Where are we going?''

Lauren fiddled with her keys. "I thought I'd take you to The Blue Whale, if that's okay.''

KC shook her head. The Blue Whale was the most

expensive restaurant on The Strand, one of Springfield's most exclusive streets.

"KC," Lauren said in her breathy, refined voice.

KC froze. Finally she met Lauren's eyes. She wondered if Lauren was going to accuse her of betrayal or berate her for setting her up.

But instead Lauren said, "I heard about what you did, how you dumped those drinks on Marielle. Thanks."

"It was the least I could do," KC mumbled. "I'm sorry about what happened."

Then there was nothing else to say. KC reached for the car door.

Lauren held up her keys. "KC, do you want to drive?"

KC wanted to ignore Lauren's offer, but she couldn't help reaching for the keys. She changed places with Lauren and slid behind the wheel.

Not looking at Lauren, KC started the car with a little too much anger. The engine roared and the clutch jerked. When KC pulled out of the parking space, they skidded a little.

"Be careful," Faith warned.

"Whoa!" giggled Winnie.

KC was still so preoccupied with the Tri Betas' injustice and with Lauren treating them to such an expensive dinner that she didn't see the other car speeding into the dorm parking lot, lights gleaming off slick pavement, screeching, heading right for them.

"KC!" Faith screamed. "There's a car coming right at you!"

"Hey," Winnie yelled. *"Look out!"*

KC's pulse went wild. For a moment she wasn't sure what was happening. The other car was a shiny, dark blur. KC shoved her foot down on the brakes and the BMW slid. There was the squeal of rubber against wet asphalt. Water flew from beneath the wheels.

"Stop!" screeched Winnie.

"Turn into the skid!" ordered Faith.

Lauren clutched her seat belt and turned even paler.

The two cars barely missed each other. KC pulled to a stop. Before any of them could say anything, the other car backed up, skidding and squealing again, until the driver's window was even with KC's. It was a vintage Corvette, perfectly restored and painted a lustrous black. The driver stuck out his head. He looked about eighteen or nineteen, and was slender with a tan, muscular arm. He fixed his eyes on KC.

"What's your problem?" KC yelled as if all her frustration could come out in one big scream.

"No problem," he came right back coolly, with a wry smile.

His coolness made KC even hotter. This guy was

ten times cockier than Buzz Off. "You're not the only person who has to drive in this parking lot!"

"I'm not?" He stuck half his torso out to look. His long, floppy hair reflected the overhead light. He shook a fist, and rattled a Rolex watch.

In her panic, KC let the clutch pop out. The engine died. She desperately tried to restart the car.

"Need a driving lesson?" he mocked.

"No, thanks," she spat back. "I'd prefer to stay alive."

"I'd prefer that, too." He laughed.

KC felt like jumping out of the car for a fistfight. But instead she concentrated on restarting Lauren's car. "And I'd prefer never to run into you again."

He gunned his engine loudly and laughed once more. "Oh, you'll run into me again. Don't you worry about that." Then the Corvette spun back around and sped off.

KC rested her face on the steering wheel. Her heart was pounding and she could barely catch her breath. "Sorry." She tried to calm herself. "Is everybody okay?"

Lauren reached over to reassure her.

KC pulled away. "I didn't see him coming. Do you still want me to drive?"

"Of course," said Lauren. "I don't mind."

"Guys," KC grumbled, forcing the BMW into gear again. "He can take his Corvette and drive off the end of the earth, for all I care. People like that make me nuts. Just because they have some fancy car, they think they own the world."

Lauren didn't say anything as KC revved the engine and drove to the most expensive restaurant on the Springfield Strand.

Two

....

Chairs squeaked against old wood. A piano lid plunked down. Pairs of jazz shoes time-stepped and hitch-kicked as singers exchanged hugs and the U of S Theater Arts Department's coffeepot gurgled dry.

Faith sat with her hands folded in her lap. Her first rehearsal for *Stop the World, I Want to Get Off* was breaking up, but Faith didn't want to stop anything. She wanted her first day of college classes to keep going and going and going.

"Thanks for your good work, everybody. It's too bad we have to break now," cheered the musical's director, junior Christopher Hammond.

The entire *Stop the World* cast wailed, their voices

echoing off the University Theater's walls. Christopher hugged his leading lady and they all cheered.

"Let's stay till midnight!"

"Let's work all night."

"Sorry," Christopher said. "You're all terrific. Start memorizing your song lyrics right away, because we'll be working on our feet tomorrow. We don't have a lot of time."

Faith didn't budge. The day had been a thrilling, racy blur: running to make it on time to Stagecraft 101, speeding back to the dorms to meet Winnie, KC, and Lauren, where they devoured leftovers from their dinner at The Blue Whale and watched their favorite soap opera, "The Best and the Beloved," panting through a beginning jazz dance class (and already feeling the ache in her thighs), making it twenty minutes early to Spanish, then having the professor toss a raw egg at her—which Faith had to name in Spanish and catch at the same time.

But as she sat in the theater Faith twisted her braid and tried to think of something to say to Christopher Hammond. She still couldn't believe he'd given her the job, even though she had sat there watching the actors and dancers in leotards and hand-knit sweaters compare dance moves and high notes. They'd been singing around a barely tuned piano on the dark stage of the University Theater. It was cold enough for mittens, and the room smelled of sawdust.

"That was great," Faith said, not sure of what else to say but feeling that she needed to offer something.

"I'll say that again," Christopher Hammond responded. He leaned over the corner of an old prop table and patted her arm. Tall and graceful, with an easy manner and a paper-white smile, he reminded Faith of an elegant TV-news anchor, or the most handsome of young city mayors.

"What?"

"You did great tonight, Faith Crowley. You're doing great." He grinned.

"Oh." Faith wasn't quite sure what to make of him. "Thank you," she stammered. "I tried to think of everything you needed. At least I figured out how to work the coffeepot." As Christopher's assistant she was getting three theater-arts credits. But she still wasn't sure what she was supposed to do.

"Don't underestimate the importance of coffee to great theatrical events."

"I won't." Faith didn't drink coffee, and yet her insides were speeding and fluttery. She'd been feeling that way all day.

"And don't underestimate your importance to *Stop The World, I Want to Get Off*, either."

Faith blushed. "Okay."

Christopher's auburn hair, still neatly combed after three hours of rehearsal was set off by a crisp white shirt and an unbuttoned vest. He smiled, and Faith felt as if an electric light had flicked on inside her.

"I'll go clean the coffeepot," she volunteered as Christopher raised his arms to gather the cast for one last pep talk.

The singers and dancers herded around the piano again, while Faith wandered into the wings, picking up used Styrofoam cups and crumpled cough-drop wrappers. Her tasks reminded her not to get too giddy about her new position. So far her job as assistant director had consisted mainly of setting up chairs and turning pages for the pianist. And yet she was still so excited that she was practically juggling coffee cups as she tossed them in the trash.

Christopher made her feel important. Of course, he had a way of making everyone feel important. Christopher was Mr. Everything. He was an athlete and big on the frat scene. He wanted to make it in TV, and even though he majored in communications, he had been given the first student musical of the year to direct. Faith knew that no matter how great Christopher said she was, she was really a small-town freshman whose theatrical experience consisted of winning high-school drama festivals and directing senior talent skits.

Faith dumped the soggy coffee grounds and unplugged the pot as Christopher made his first end-of-rehearsal speech.

"Great sing- and read-through," Christopher encouraged.

"Let's open tomorrow," kidded Kimberly, the friendly black dancer who lived next door to Faith in the dorms. She did a tap step and ended with an arm outstretched.

Everyone laughed, and soon there was an impromptu chorus of " 'You're the top . . .' "

Merideth, the stage manager, clapped his hands and demanded order in his mock-fierce, humorous voice. "We have to be out of the building by ten, so everybody listen up. You can all act like drama majors after you leave."

Faith had met Merideth during orientation week. He was actually the one who'd suggested she become Christopher's assistant director. Faith liked Merideth. He was a teddy-bearish sophomore and ran things with a cynical efficiency. She recognized others, mostly from Coleridge Hall, her creative-arts dorm, and was amazed as every song revealed a more melodic voice, a spicier personality. In comparison, Faith felt like bland Wonder Bread.

"Quiet, everyone," Christopher announced. "Unfortunately we're just the little student musical this semester. The opera department has first dibs on the theater for their production of *Hansel and Gretel,* so I'm afraid we're going to have to perform on their set."

There was a collective grumble at how inappropriate that backdrop would be for their stark, stylized musical. The back of the stage was already draped with large, corny backdrops showing a fairy-tale woods.

"We won't worry about the backdrops for a while," Christopher told them. "We'll just rehearse our musical, and figure out later how to make it all work together. Just think about *Stop the World,* and don't worry about *Hansel and Gretel* for the time being. Remember to bring in all your ideas. I want to hear from everybody. I'm so glad to have you all on board."

"Anyone forgets their script," Merideth tossed out as he dimmed the lights, "and they have to buy doughnuts for the rest of us all semester."

Faith made sure to pick up her script and score. By the time she'd put away the coffeepot and made sure all the trash was collected, everyone was gone—everyone except Christopher, who was sitting at the prop table scribbling on a yellow legal pad.

It was quiet. Only one light was still on, a single work light that cast shadows like a street lamp. Faith tiptoed through the puddle of light, hurrying out.

"Faith," Christopher called.

Faith was at the door, her hand poised over the wide crash bar. She turned back. Her heart, already beating faster, jolted up another notch. "Yes?"

Christopher kept writing, not looking up. "Could you do a few things for me before tomorrow night?"

"Of course. I'm your assistant. Whatever you need."

He ripped the paper off the pad and held it out to her. "Can you handle all this?"

Faith walked back through the slant of light to read his list. *Proof the publicity blurb. Get measurements for the costume department.*

"No problem."

"You know, I don't expect you to just make coffee. I want to hear your ideas, too."

"Okay," Faith said quickly, heading back to the door, past some cut-out *Hansel and Gretel* trees, over the floor dotted with uneven bits of tape.

"Good night," Christopher called out. "You really are doing great."

"Yeah, sure," Faith giggled to herself, grinning. She ran down the hall and out the side door. It was pitch-black out, a misty and cold night. "Great coffee maker. Great chair folder. I'm sure you can't wait to find out about all the other great things I can do."

Tap, tap, tap, tap, tap.
Ding!
Tap, tap, tap, tap, tap . . .
Winnie stood in the doorway to her dorm room

feeling weary and overwhelmed. At the end of what seemed like an endless first day of classes, she was greeted by the relentless typing of her roommate, Melissa McDormand, on an old manual typewriter.

Winnie waited in the doorway, hoping for a *hello,* a *how ya doin'?*, or even *can I borrow your shampoo?* But instead all she got was *tap, tap, tap.* Already Melissa was a term-paper machine.

Winnie was unable to keep herself from humming and stamping her purple boots. Their room was in Forest Hall, a brand-new dorm with a jock party reputation. With its cottage-cheese ceilings and orange racing stripes, the dorm was usually referred to as "the motel." Down the coed hall, stereos were blasting and some football players were splattering water balloons against the wall. But as far as fast-typing Melissa was concerned, the ruckus, the pranks—even Winnie herself—were no distraction at all.

"Hi," Winnie finally said, pulling the door shut with a hollow *thwack.* She dumped her books on her bed. It was a huge stack, since she'd already checked out extra reading assignments after her first sessions of French Conversation and Logic 1. After getting so crazed over Josh during orientation week, Winnie had decided to get serious for a change. She was bending over backward to get a good start with her classes. Still, when she looked at all those thick volumes, she wanted to crawl under her blankets and sleep until next term.

"Oh. Hello." Melissa looked up briefly, then went right back to her typing again. Her straight red hair was tied up in a careless short ponytail. She was wearing a U of S track suit.

"Hello," Winnie whispered. "Hello, hello. *Bon jour*."

That first orientation week, Winnie and Melissa had gotten into an awful argument after Winnie had drunk rum and passed out in Josh's room, then came back to her room and made lots of noise. She and Melissa had made up, but the relationship between them was still far from cozy. If Josh hadn't lived on her floor, Winnie might have gone back out and studied in the hall. But, at this point, she wanted to face Josh even less than she wanted to be cooped up with Melissa.

Gee, hi, Josh. So great to see you. Maybe I can sit and watch while you do some hacking on your computer.

Winnie didn't know where else to go. She'd left KC at the magazine stack in the library. Faith was probably still at rehearsal. And even after that fancy dinner the night before—maybe *because* of that fancy dinner—Winnie felt uncomfortable about trying to get to know Lauren. So, no matter how intimidating Melissa was, Winnie was stuck with her.

Winnie walked over to her half of the sterile beige

room, where she'd tacked a fishnet on her wall. It gave the dorm room a sea-grotto feel, and Winnie had stowed her incense, horror novels, bubble gum, jewelry, weird newspaper clippings, and other bizarre belongings in little pockets here and there on the netting.

"Gee, Winnie," Winnie projected, talking out loud to herself because she was in no mood to be ignored. "You've kept your half of the room clean for two whole days. I was sure you were going to be a total slob after the way things started out during orientation week."

Winnie lowered her voice to answer herself. She felt like a ventriloquist. "That's okay, Melissa. I figured that since we had to live together, I'd try and make it so we could get along. And I think we will get along, if we can just talk to each other more than two seconds each day."

The tapping slowed down. *Tap . . . tap.*

"Of course, Melissa, we could just go back to our cold war. Hey, maybe that would help me understand my Western Civ class, which I start tomorrow. The origin of conflict."

The tapping stopped altogether.

But Winnie's mouth was on overdrive. There was no stopping it. "Now my mother, who's a therapist, always says it's better to get things totally out in the open, which is just what I'm trying to do. Of course, my mother is often wrong about things. Like she thinks I need to figure out everything for myself, so she never stops me from making big mistakes, like getting so drunk during orientation.''

Winnie collapsed on the floor, limbs outspread. "God, I'm a motor mouth. Shut me up, Melissa. Save me from myself."

Melissa took off her reading glasses, and placed them on her dresser, next to an anatomy model and an old, pill-covered sweater.

"Sorry," Melissa finally said. "I had to get all my lecture notes typed up." She smiled. "Winnie, do you always talk this much?"

"Usually," Winnie admitted, sitting up. "Except at five in the morning, like the first time we yakked. That tends to be my quiet time."

"I'm glad."

Usually Melissa was at track workout or in the library, and so at first Winnie had referred to her as the invisible, mystery roommate. But now that she took a good look at Melissa's square, tanned face, hard brown eyes, determined mouth, and taut runner's body, she saw that there was nothing mysterious about her. More and more she realized that Melissa was as solid and formidable as a brick wall.

In comparison, Winnie felt like a Christmas tree ornament.

"I know I'm acting kind of weird," Winnie said

in a less manic voice. "But I figure we're pretty mismatched as roommates. Still, I think we can get to be friends. Otherwise this room could be a torture chamber again."

Melissa turned around in her chair.

Winnie picked out one of her books for Logic 1. "I just don't think I can handle another argument with you this semester. Not with logic to think about." She slapped her forehead. "Why did I ever sign up for a class in logic? Me, the world's most illogical person. What was I thinking of?"

"What *were* you thinking of?" Melissa wanted to know. She was sitting backward in her desk chair, facing Winnie, her chin on the backrest.

Winnie shrugged. "Good question." Winnie scrambled back up to her bed, feeling a little foolish but more relaxed. "Why do I do a lot of things? My friends from home, Faith and KC, they ask that, too. But you haven't met them. So you don't know whom I'm talking about." When Melissa stared as if Winnie were a high hurdle, Winnie couldn't resist tossing back some of her roommate's straightforward honesty. "Are you always this serious?"

"Serious isn't the same thing as humorless," Melissa clarified.

"Oh."

Melissa smiled. "I'm sorry, Winnie. I don't mean to ignore you. I just have a lot of things to think about and sometimes it's hard for me to change gears." Even her voice was clear and determined. "I'm on an athletic scholarship. But just because I'm a good college runner, I can't assume there's a great job waiting for me out there as a pro. So I'd like to get into med school. And if I don't work like a maniac, I'll never make it. Do you know what I mean?"

"I think I'm beginning to."

Melissa nodded. "So what's your future?"

"What?" Winnie felt defensive. Even KC was a softie compared to Melissa.

"Why are you here? You must want more than just to party, like everyone else in this dorm."

Winnie stared. She realized it was impolite, but she was beginning to feel fascinated. KC's ambition didn't really appeal to her, because it was so concerned with money and status. But there was something about Melissa's strong determination that filled her with admiration—and made her feel like a knothead in comparison.

"I don't know why I'm here," Winnie heard herself admit. "Not that I'm not smart. I was smart enough to skip a year in grade school." She made a face. "I told you that so you'd know there was a good reason for my immaturity."

"I see."

Winnie instantly felt embarrassed. Boasting about

being a child whiz was pretty lame, especially since her great promise had turned into a sea of under-achievement. "But I'm not sure what I want to do now. I mean, my classes today were confusing."

"In what way?"

"Not French. I liked that." Winnie shook her earrings. "But logic? And tomorrow I have my first class in criminal justice. Why did I sign up for that?"

"Why don't you drop logic?" Melissa suggested. "Take something you're really interested in instead."

"Can I do that?"

"Of course. You can drop and switch classes almost until midterms. As long as another class still has room, you can transfer."

"Really? Maybe I will. I know you think I'm the queen of flakes, and that may be true, but I really want to get more serious, now that classes are starting. Believe it or not, being a full-time lightweight can be pretty tiring."

Melissa laughed.

"So I guess tomorrow I'll drop logic and take something else. Like home ec."

Melissa frowned.

"Just a joke, Melissa. A joke."

"I know it's a joke." Melissa put her glasses back on. "Actually, I kind of liked home ec in high school. It was the one class where I didn't worry about being the best. I could just kick back and be happy with sewing the world's ugliest gym bag."

Winnie stared at her no-longer-mysterious roommate with new warmth. "You should have tasted my Tuna Surprise."

"Mine was worse." Melissa smiled and went back to her tapping.

New Beginnings.

That was the theme of the first weekly dinner for the pledges of the Tri Beta sorority house. As Lauren found her place card that same Monday night and slipped into her chair decorated with sprigs of thyme and little daisies, she thought about what a strange beginning it was. It felt more like a terminal dead end.

"Welcome, Lauren," said Courtney Conner, the Tri Beta president, in her honey voice. Her blond hair was perfectly combed, held back by a velvet headband that set off her lace-trimmed smock. She matched the sorority house dining room, which was decorated in springlike yellows and greens.

"Hello," Lauren said. She was thinking back to the night before, how she'd wanted to buy Faith, Winnie, and KC's friendship by taking them to a fancy restaurant. And how her mother's donation, worth a few hundred Blue Whale dinners, had bought a place in the sorority for her.

Courtney leaned over the chair next to Lauren while pledges fluttered around, all excited and over-dressed. Perfume hung in the air like fog. "I'm pleased that you finally decided to join our house. I know it must have been a difficult decision for you."

Lauren shrugged.

"We thought a lot about how to make you feel at home here, and I hope we succeed," Courtney assured her. "We're very glad to have you on board." With a smile, Courtney moved on, like the hostess at an elegant society affair.

Lauren sat fiddling with her place card, wishing that she could lift herself magically out of the sorority house and disappear. She would rather have been back in the dorm doing something she really cared about—like working on her writing. She was in the midst of a daydream about writing a great novel that would expose college rites for what they were when she felt someone sit down next to her.

"Hello, Lauren."

Lauren nearly gagged. It was Marielle. Thin, button-nosed Marielle, with her hair parted on one side and her charm bracelet, rattling, had tortured and humiliated Lauren all through rush.

"Hi."

"Welcome to Tri Beta." Marielle crossed her legs and leaned over the table. "I'm going to be your big sister."

"You?"

"Courtney and I talked about this for a long time." Marielle threw an impatient glance at Courtney, who paused from welcoming another pledge to glance back with maternal approval.

"You did?"

"Yes." Marielle checked her manicure. "First, I have to apologize if I was a little rough during rush. I only do that to test girls, to see if they're really Tri Beta material. You know that, don't you?"

"I know," Lauren mumbled.

Marielle continued, with pumped-up cheer, "But now, since it's been decided that you *are* Tri Beta material, I want to make things up to you."

"You do?"

The dinner was being called to order. Girls took their places as sheets listing the letters in the Greek alphabet were passed around the table. Lauren took a page from Marielle, then passed the rest along.

Marielle leaned into Lauren and whispered as Courtney asked the girls to read the Greek letters out loud. "When we get done with this, Lauren, you and I can talk about what we need to do to make you into the best Tri Beta possible, the Tri Beta I know you can be."

Lauren nodded and stared at the Greek letters.

"There are a lot of things that can make a big dif-

ference. Hair. Clothes. Weight. We can work on all
of them together."

"Alpha," Lauren recited. "Beta."

"How does that sound, Lauren?"

"Delta, gamma . . ." Lauren cringed. She could
hardly wait.

Three

······················

"hat's all for our first session," Dr. Hermann, the Western Civ professor, said in closing. "Read the chapter on ancient Egypt for Thursday. Quizzes will pop up, so be prepared."

There was a moan from the class. Books snapped shut. People began hopping up from their seats. The two-hundred-seat circular hall came to life, talk spreading like wildfire as the professor shut off the overhead projector and began reeling in the electrical cord.

Immediately KC began heading for the aisle.

"Where to now?" Winnie asked, digging her chin into KC's shoulder as they waited for the crowd to chug along. Faith stood behind her. And behind

Faith, Lauren shuffled along with her notebook held tightly against her chest. Western Civ was the one class all four girls had in common.

Faith fished a sheet of yellow legal paper out of her jeans pocket and read it over. "I have to go over to the costume shop and drop off some measurements for *Stop the World*. KC, why are you in such a hurry?"

KC clung to her briefcase. "I have another class right away. It's the discussion group for my Intro to Business class."

"Discussion group?" Winnie wrinkled her nose.

KC nodded. "Big lectures on Mondays, and then we meet in smaller groups with a teaching assistant on Tuesdays, Thursdays, and Fridays. It's a heavy-duty course."

"I guess I won't transfer into that class." Winnie wove her arm through KC's and Faith's as the three of them trotted up the stairs.

Lauren followed, hugging her heavy books and saying nothing.

When they hit the busy corridor, Winnie and Faith waved and headed in the direction of the theater-arts complex, while KC strode in the opposite direction. She walked quickly in high heels, swinging her briefcase as if she were headed to a board meeting or a debate final.

Lauren struggled to keep up, past the geography department bulletin board and a big advertisement for student tours to Scandinavia. They made their way through the crowded corridor until both of them pushed through the double doors.

It was bright out and cold. Staying a few steps ahead of Lauren, KC ran down stone steps and wound her way between the library and Parker Hall. KC wasn't sure why Lauren continued to follow her. The paths that crisscrossed around campus were glutted with students rushing and biking.

"Lauren, where are you headed?" KC asked as she stopped to check her campus map. But when KC looked down, she was suddenly embarrassed. She was wearing the expensive black dress that she and Lauren had bought during rush. KC had borrowed Lauren's credit card to pay for the dress and had not yet paid her back. And since she'd lost her job, she didn't know when or how she was ever going to pay Lauren back.

"Nowhere." Lauren trailed as KC took off again, trotting up the steps to Parker Hall, the business-administration building. "My English Lit class isn't for two hours. And I had creative writing lab early this morning."

They passed a couple of computer labs. Finally KC ducked into the ladies' room. Lauren followed her in there, too.

They were the only ones in front of the mirror. KC saw Lauren's sad, pale face, framed by a tweedy beige sweater and a little lace collar. In comparison, KC looked as dark and exotic as a perfect purple rose.

"KC," Lauren began, biting her lip and looking down, "I know it's kind of weird that I joined the sorority and you didn't."

"It's not weird at all," KC came back too quickly, redoing her lipstick and neatening her hair. She wanted to be totally together for her business class, and that meant not being distracted by her confusing feelings about Lauren and rush and the money she owed for her only good dress.

"I'm glad you feel that way."

"Look, Lauren, I know I still owe you money for charging this dress on your credit card," KC finally came back defensively. "I'm sorry. I don't have a job right now, but I'll pay you back as soon as I can. It's just that I can't think about getting another job just yet. My classes are turning out to be really hard. Just for Intro to Business I have to do two papers and a group research project."

"Don't worry." Lauren looked like she was the one in debt. "I know you lost your job because you stuck up for me. I don't expect you to pay me back for the dress."

"Really?" KC felt an incredible surge of relief. "Are you serious?"

Lauren nodded.

KC wasn't sure what to say. She saw the hurt in

Lauren's eyes, the need still to be friends. She wished she could undo everything awful that had happened between them, but she didn't know how to put those feelings together with her own insecurity and regret. "Lauren, thanks. That's really generous of you. You're always generous. I really appreciate it. I know this whole thing isn't your fault."

At that moment, three more girls walked in, laughing and imitating one of their professors. KC put away her lipstick and brush.

Lauren grabbed KC's hand, as if she were afraid KC were going to run away. "KC, if you have to go job hunting again, you can borrow my car. But don't worry about it for now. Getting a good start in your classes is more important."

"Thanks." KC started for the door, then turned back and gave Lauren a big hug. "Thanks a lot."

"Anytime," Lauren whispered and followed KC into the hall.

"The business of business is business."

The nasal-voiced teaching assistant, a graduate student named Naomi Potemkin, stood in front of a small, ordinary classroom. There was a TV and VCR in one corner and a table up front stacked high with business magazines. The smell of chalk hung in the air. Naomi looked around at her Intro to Business discussion group to see if they understood what she was talking about.

KC understood what Naomi meant. She'd understood at the professor's introductory lecture the day before. She'd understood the night before when she'd devoured every word of the first reading assignment. Business was about making things work, about providing something that people wanted to buy, about creating wealth. And she knew that business wasn't easy. Unlike getting into a sorority—which just seemed to depend on connections and money— business demanded desire, smarts, and sheer back-breaking work.

But the other students in KC's discussion group were wishy-washy. KC wanted to stand up and yell at them. *Maybe this doesn't really mean much to you. Maybe your parents are great businesspeople and have tons of money to buy you cars and computers and ski-lift tickets. Maybe you can buy your way into prestigious sorority houses and private clubs. Maybe you've never seen your parents running a crummy little health-food restaurant, limping by, barely making it year after year.*

"The purpose of this discussion group is to bring up different points of view," Naomi instructed. "And to work on our group research projects. Who wants to comment on yesterday's lecture?"

No one had the nerve to go first. Girls folded their

hands. Guys looked at their track shoes. Someone closed the cover of a book.

KC couldn't contain herself any longer. Her hand shot up. Maybe the other freshmen wanted to sit around like lumps, but she didn't.

"Yes. Can you give me your name?" Naomi peered over her glasses.

"KC Angeletti." KC noticed Naomi make a pencil mark in the attendance roster. Good. Maybe she would get extra points for being the first to speak.

"I was struck by something I read in *The New York Times*," KC said, her heart beating hard. The other students stared at her. "So much energy goes into acquiring companies and moving stock around, instead of figuring out how to make new things that people want to buy. I'd like to research starting a small business—how you find something to make or sell and where you go from there."

"Good idea," Naomi said. "What do the rest of you think about that?"

As soon as KC began to enjoy a surge of self-satisfaction, other hands shot up. Naomi called on a guy in the corner seat right next to the door. He stood up, his tall frame propped cockily against his desk. KC gawked even though she tried not to. She didn't know how she could have missed seeing him before.

He stared right at KC. "I say think big, not small.

To write off big business is incredibly naive." He spoke confidently, like he wasn't used to being interrupted. "And the stock market supports business in this country. If it weren't for corporations, this country would be a country of mom-and-pop grocery stores. *Poor* mom-and-pop grocery stores." When he was done, he leaned back against his desk chair as if it were the cornerstone of his thousand-acre estate.

A surge of rage burned through KC. She still couldn't believe she hadn't noticed him the second she'd walked in! She had figured that she would see his overconfident, mocking face sometime on campus. She just had hoped that it wouldn't be so soon. Mr. Overconfident, Obnoxious, Sparkly-black-Corvette!

"Oh, I'm Steven Garth," he added. He folded his lean body and, just as he sat back down, turned his head to wink at KC.

"Ugh," KC whispered, clutching the sides of her desk.

"Thank you, Steven," said Naomi. "Who else supports Mr. Garth's point of view?" She pointed to a surfer type in the back row. "How about you, sir?"

The surfer floundered, but KC no longer felt A-student superior. She kept her eyes on the front blackboard, which wasn't easy considering that Steven's gaze and his half-mocking smile were now glued to her left cheekbone. KC sensed that he'd been staring at her since the class began.

As other students finally joined the discussion, KC couldn't help turning her head just enough to look back at Steven Garth through the protection of a few stray curls. That same clever gleam was in his eyes. He was definitely an irritating kind of handsome. His smile was too perfect and his eyelashes too long, giving a false softness to his otherwise lean, aristocratic face. His straight hair flopped over his forehead, so that every few minutes he had to flick it back. The designer emblem had been ripped off his polo shirt, leaving a telltale ragged hole. He didn't wear socks, even though it was cold out, and he just kept staring at KC, that blatant arrogance burning in his eyes.

Naomi guided the conversation back to research projects. "That's also what our smaller class groups are about—dividing up and forming teams. Since teamwork is an essential part of any business, we feel that it's important that your research project for this course be collective. I'm going to divide you into six sections of four students each."

Naomi quickly counted people off by location, and then chairs and desks were scooted together. KC was relieved to be sitting far away from Steven Garth and tried to focus on her group, which included a guy from Kuwait whose English was difficult to understand, a back-to-school grandmother, and a football jock she recognized from Winnie's dorm.

But a moment later Steven was there, too, looming over KC. He was so close that she could breathe in his expensive aftershave.

Steven fished a twenty-dollar bill out of his pocket and waved it in front of the jock. "Trade research groups with you."

Quick as nothing, the jock took the bill with a silly grin and sidled over to the corner group.

Steven slid down in the chair next to KC.

"You have some nerve!" KC objected.

"It's just capitalism in action," Steven said.

They locked eyes, waiting as Naomi strolled by. When no one mentioned Steven's little bribe to the TA, KC waited to see who would take charge of the group.

Steven planted himself on a desktop, his elbows on his knees, and started to lecture. "So what do we want to do? Study General Motors? IBM? I say forget either of those."

"What?" KC flared up.

He patted her shoulder, as if she were a Little Leaguer who'd just lost the final game. KC jerked away from his touch.

"There must be a better idea," he said. "A more innovative approach."

"Of course there's a better idea," KC intruded. "And I've got it."

The foreign student, whose name was Edward, looked confused.

Helen, the grandmother, smiled. "What is it?"

KC was bluffing. No idea was in her head, but she prayed that if she kept talking, a decent notion would come to her. "What I'm saying—if Mr. Garth lets me say it—is, why study someone else's business, big *or* small?"

"I thought that's what we were supposed to do," said Helen.

Edward nodded.

Steven was leaning back, waiting for KC to create her own mess and drown in it. But more words flew out of KC's mouth before she even knew what she really meant. "Let's create our own business," she said.

"No, no," Edward reacted.

Helen frowned.

Steven's mocking smile turned a little less threatening as something new entered into it. There was a trace of interest, a tinge of respect.

KC tried to ignore him and forged ahead. "If we want to be like every other dope in this class, we can read some best-seller about the one-second manager and give our book reports. Or we can really learn. Really do something. We can create some kind of small business—anything—that we operate for the term, and have that be our project. I bet Naomi would okay it.''

Edward looked even more mystified and Helen had *no* written all over her face until Steven leaned forward on his desktop.

''I bet she will,'' he said.

''What?''

''Okay your idea, Angeletti. I bet she will.'' Then Steven tossed back his hair and got that gleam in his eyes again. ''Especially when I figure out just what kind of venture for us to do.''

''Wait a minute,'' KC objected. ''Who said you get to choose what kind of business we start?''

Steven looked more pleased with himself. ''You were the one who decided not to do a book report. I was just following your example.''

''What happened to teamwork?''

''You were the one who had the great idea.''

Helen's and Edward's heads were swinging back and forth as if they were watching a tennis match.

''Fine.'' KC held up her hand firmly. ''How about if we each bring in an idea for a business next time, and then we'll vote? If we can't all agree on something, we'll do dumb book reports like everyone else. Okay?''

Edward nodded and Helen shrugged.

Steven just kept staring at KC so intently that she

thought he would burn a hole through her skin. "So you really think you can pull this off, Angeletti?"

"Yes, Garth," she shot back. "I do."

"Well, well. I'd certainly like to see it."

"Well, that's hunky-dory. Because this has nothing to do with you."

"But I'm your business partner, Angeletti. Your fellow entrepreneur. Your teammate."

"And that undoubtedly will be my biggest problem."

By that time the desks were being shuffled around again, and it was time for class to break up. Helen and Edward were already on their way out, waving and promising to have ideas to contribute when they met again.

Quickly, KC gathered up her books and headed for the door. But she wasn't quick enough. Steven was on her heels.

"Little angel," she heard him scoff on the way out. She whipped around. "What!"

"I bet Angeletti means 'little angel.' " He blocked her path as she tried to make it into the hall, and laughed.

"What does Garth mean?" KC snapped. "What are you, heir to Garth Petroleum or something?"

"One of the heirs." For the first time his expressive, mocking face showed nothing. For that one second his glittering eyes went dead.

"What a sorry coincidence," KC said, trying to hide her shock. She hadn't been serious about Garth Petroleum. It was just the comeback that had popped into her head. Steven wasn't just rich. He was unbelievably rich. No wonder he was such a conceited, arrogant jerk.

"Coincidence?"

"Just like us meeting in this class is a sorry coincidence," KC rambled. "After you practically ran over my friends and me the other night. I guess that's because you figure if you own the gasoline, you own the road. All the roads."

"No coincidence," Steven came back. "I followed you out of Western Civ. I told you when I saw you in the BMW that we were going to meet again." He grinned. "Good thing there was room for me to transfer into Intro to Business. And after the way you drive, and the harebrained ideas you bring up, I think you might need some help."

Four

The next afternoon was breezy. The tops of the evergreen trees did little hula dances in the wind. The sun spiked through the clouds, making shadows play across the brick pathways and deep-green lawns.

It was the perfect day to jog, and Winnie had talked Faith and KC into joining her at the track for what she called an obsessive, face-the-facts-about-your-thighs fitness run.

But on the way, Faith had given in to an obsession of her own. Or maybe it was an impulse. She never used to follow impulses, but that time, for some crazy reason, she ducked inside the theater's scenery shop. As she was leaving the power saws, the cans of paint, and the rolls of canvas she ran smack into Christopher Hammond.

"Faith. What are you doing here?"

Faith felt like a fool. "I was, oh, just looking over the old scenery pieces they have lying around."

"What for?" Christopher's forehead wrinkled up. "For my show?"

She shrugged.

"You decided to look through the scenery pieces on your own?" he clarified as they left the smell of glue and wood chips behind and wandered out in the direction of Mill Pond.

Faith cleared her throat and clutched her books to her chest. "I'm sorry. I should have asked you before I went into the scenery shop, but I was just walking by on my way to meet my friends, and—well, it was a spur-of-the-moment kind of thing."

"That's great." He stayed by her side as she drifted toward the athletic fields. "So tell me, what scenery do you think we could use?"

"I'm sure you don't want to know my dumb opinion. I don't even know why I went in there. It's not part of my job."

Christopher stopped, sticking his hands in the pocket of his sport coat. "Faith, I told you, I don't expect you to just make coffee. Tell me what scenery you think we can use. Or do I have to assign you to tell me after our next rehearsal?"

"You really want to know what I think?"

"That's why I asked."

"Well, okay." Faith scuffed her cowboy boots against the ground and took a deep breath. "I thought since we have to work against the *Hansel and Gretel* backdrops—I know you don't want to deal with that yet, but I keep thinking about it even though it's not my job—anyway, I thought maybe the scene shop had some, you know, neutral boxes, to use as chairs or benches or trees—as everything. See, if the set pieces were simple and kind of abstract, then maybe the backdrops wouldn't matter."

When Christopher didn't respond immediately, she added. "I know it's a terrible idea. I might not have even told you if I hadn't run into you."

"You wouldn't?"

"I was just checking into it, to report back to you and let you know," Faith backtracked.

Christopher really took her in. He laughed and patted her shoulder. His hand lingered just a little, then slid lightly down her arm. "Faith, if you come up with a solution that I haven't thought of, all the better. Two heads are better than one."

"You really think that?"

"Really."

"Thanks."

"Thank *you*."

Luckily Faith didn't have to say anything else because they resumed walking, past Mill Pond and into the crowd heading off campus. It seemed that every third person recognized Christopher. She remembered Merideth calling him "Sir Christopher" and joking that people would bow to him if it had been the custom.

"Hi, Chris. Great to see you."

"Christopher. How's everything at ODT?"

"Yo, Hammond."

Girls glanced back long after they passed. Guys nodded with respect. Walking with Christopher was like taking a stroll with a movie star.

Faith had barely realized that she'd reached the turnoff for the track-and-field complex when she spotted Winnie and KC in the distance. It was not in her nature to keep friends waiting, and yet she lingered at the crossroads.

Christopher stalled, too. He took a long sip from a stone drinking fountain, then leaned back for a moment against the fence that surrounded the tennis courts.

"See, Faith, I have this theory about doing theater, or running a fraternity, or anything, for that matter. My theory is, don't try and do everything yourself. Assume that everyone has something positive to offer. Give people lots of rope."

"And you don't think they'll hang themselves?"

"I think they'll build stronger ladders."

Faith wasn't sure how long she stood there, staring at Christopher's auburn hair being tousled by the breeze. The world had slowed down. Nothing was happening, she told herself, except that she was probably standing with her mouth open, like the dorky freshman she was. And yet she was unable to get her legs to take her in another direction, away from the aura of Christopher's thoughtful smile and gracious eyes.

"I like to be open to other people's inputs," he went on. "The first few weeks of this quarter are going to be nuts for me. I'm carrying twenty credit hours. I'm a big brother to new pledges at the fraternity. And the TV station in town is interviewing for an intern." He clenched his fists. "I'd sure like to be the one they pick. It's the only way to get a foot in the door for TV. I'm on their final list, but I have to show them some practical work. That's one of the reasons I pushed to do this show."

"The people from the TV station will come and see *Stop the World?*" Faith managed to ask.

"A rehearsal. I won't know when. All I know is, they're picking the intern before we actually open the show. I have a lot riding on this. And I really appreciate your help."

Faith's heart did a double pump. She only half took in Winnie, running toward her in huge satin shorts and a torn black sweatshirt. KC, in a gray U of S sweatshirt, waited further back.

They both were yelling.

"Faith! Face the facts about those thighs!"

"Come on, Faith. I have homework to do!"

"My friends," Faith explained, not budging and feeling embarrassed again.

"So I see." He backed up and smiled. "See you at rehearsal tonight."

"See you tonight." Faith stood stock-still, unable to move until Christopher had completely disappeared.

Finally Faith joined KC and Winnie and the three of them were jogging on the black cinder track, looping round and round while athletes practiced pole vaulting and long jumps inside the oval.

"Can you believe that attitude?" Faith was asking. "He's amazing. Most directors would have yelled at me for making a suggestion like that. But he respects everyone who works with him. Christopher even trusts me."

"Faith, why shouldn't he trust you? You're only the most responsible person in the entire world."

"As usual, Winnie, you're understating things," KC said sarcastically. She held her stomach and pretended to be ready to throw up. "Like how much fun it would be to run around in circles."

"It *is* fun, KC. It's Zen."

"Win, you should use all this energy for something productive, not running around like a rat in a cage."

"Yeah?" Winnie huffed in and out, counting as she breathed. "Hey, maybe that's the class I should transfer into. Zen rodentology." She pumped her knees high, hopping in double-time and surging out front. "Do you think that's my problem? Maybe I run off all my productive energy, so I can't concentrate on more important things. Of course, Melissa runs, too, and look at her. But she's a distance runner. She goes over hills and dales, across mountains and streams, through forests . . ."

"Winnie, I'm kidding! I'm sure you could do whatever you wanted to do," KC insisted.

"As long as I could figure out what that was." Winnie waited for KC and Faith to catch up. They ran in stride again. "Anyway, back to Mr. Wonderful."

"I never called him Mr. Wonderful."

"Mr. Generous, he loves your suggestions."

Faith didn't laugh. "I keep thinking about Brooks, and how things with him were always the way I expected them to be because he's so sure of everything, so in control. I guess I assumed that all guys were like that. But Christopher keeps surprising me. From the first second I met him, he's never done what I expected. He's even up for this internship at the local TV station. He's—"

Suddenly Winnie and KC closed in on her. Each laced an arm through one of Faith's.

Faith clammed up.

"KC, are you thinking what I'm thinking?" Winnie teased.

"I hope not." KC smiled.

"What?" Faith asked, innocent as ever.

"Oh, nothing," Winnie sang. "I know, I'm the only one of this trio who has guys on the brain."

KC interrupted, "And maybe that's why you can't concentrate."

Winnie picked up the pace and rolled her eyes. "I just mean, Faith, it sounds an awful lot to me like you've bounced back from the breakup with Brooks."

Faith pushed hair out of her eyes. "Why do you say that? I can barely stand thinking about it. He won't even talk to me. It's horrible."

"But I'm not talking about Brooks," Winnie said, pretending to hop on Faith's toes. "I'm talking about your true-confession feelings for Mr. Wonderful."

"What?" Suddenly Faith shot out in front with a giggle and a shriek. *"Noooooo!"* Her braid flapped behind her and her face grew very red. "Look!" she screamed, running back and around her old friends, "it's not even an issue. He's older. He's a frat bigwig. There's probably a rule against guys like him dating a girl who isn't in a sorority. So even if I have had a few passing thoughts and fantasies . . ."

Winnie pumped her arms and screeched, "You admit it! You've fallen for a Bee Moc. You admit it!"

KC pulled both of them off the track and flopped over her knees. She was heaving for breath. "A what?"

"A Bee Moc," Winnie explained, not panting at all. "Big man on campus. B.M.O.C. Bee Moc."

"Got it." When KC lifted her head again, she looked deadly serious, even though she still had to gulp for breath. "Whatever he is, don't lose your head, Faith. You're on the rebound. Even though you were the one to end things with Brooks, don't underestimate how long it'll take for you to get over him."

Winnie giggled. "I've always found that falling for another guy is the perfect way to get over someone else."

KC ignored her. "And more important, Faith, we're just starting college. We need to think about accomplishing things and getting good grades, not distracting ourselves from our goals. No offense, Win, but what you went through with Josh during orientation is a perfect example. Look how it distracted you!"

KC looked away from Faith and Winnie and began to lecture more urgently, almost as if she were talking to herself. "Guys are just a distraction, an annoying, stupid distraction from what's really important! I've had it with them. They think they can say whatever they want, do whatever they—" KC suddenly seemed to realize that she was giving a speech. She threw up her hands and then folded onto the bottom bleacher. "Oh, forget it."

Winnie and Faith stood staring at KC, both with their hands on their hips, baffled, unsure what to make of her outburst.

"Hit a nerve?" Winnie insinuated.

KC didn't answer.

"I won't get distracted. Don't worry about me," Faith said as she went over and sat next to KC.

Winnie stayed on the track, bending and stretching at the waist. "I'm not so sure it's you she's worried about. 'Fess up, KC. Did somebody accost you in accounting class this morning?"

"No!"

"Did he ask you to come back to his dorm room and look over his spreadsheets?"

"Winnie! You're the one who has guys on the brain, not me."

"Okay."

After that they all stared off in different directions. Winnie stretched her calf muscles. Faith stared up at the sky with a dreamy smile. KC put her chin in her hands.

"Let's head back to the dorms," KC said after a while. "I have to think up an idea for my business project." Before Winnie or Faith could argue, she was leading the way through the gate and out by way of the athletic fields.

Faith flew after her. She was almost lightheaded. And it wasn't from the jogging. She felt as if she could run forever, which was pretty bizarre considering that Winnie was the runner and Faith was more inclined to ride horses or go for mountain hikes. She knew that KC had been trying to warn her, but the speech had only made her feel even more hopeful. Not that she was hopeful about Christopher—she was too realistic for that. But she was willing to pour herself into Christopher's production. Rather than being a distraction, the play was about learning and changing, gathering experience, and tackling things that were new.

Faith was feeling so airy and optimistic that she barely realized she'd started running again until she slammed into both Winnie and KC. The two of them had suddenly stopped at the edge of the soccer field.

"Oops. Sorry."

"That's okay."

"What are you two staring at? Win? KC?"

"Nothing."

"Let's go."

"Oh." Faith felt her high-flying optimism drop like a broken elevator.

Winnie wiggled nervously and hummed.

"Do you want to go another way?"

A pack of students were practicing soccer moves on the nearest field, running, and kicking in orderly formation. Faith recognized several people from the dorms. And there was no mistaking the freshman leading the drill. Especially since Faith had known him since eighth grade.

Brooks.

Brooks was so familiar to her. His determined body was strong from rock climbing, and he ran after the ball, angrily stabbing at it with his feet, his curly hair flying. He wore two T-shirts layered over each other, each of which Faith recognized. One was his old high school–baseball jersey; the other she'd given him when he tried out for the pre-Olympic soccer team when he was fifteen. Memories rushed into Faith's brain—sweet, eerie, and horribly painful, all at once.

"Brooks is head of the intramural soccer league. I guess they're having practice," Winnie said. "I forgot to tell you about it."

KC nodded. "We figured you wouldn't be too eager to join a team."

"Really."

And then it happened, just the way it had happened over the last few days. Brooks stopped playing and, as if he'd been alerted to Faith's presence by ESP, looked in her direction. A flash of rage was in his eyes, and he seemed to look through her as if she were an open window.

Winnie started to talk again, trying to distract Faith from Brooks's accusing glare. "I think KC is right," she rambled. "Let's forget about guys. Let's wipe Brooks and Josh and Mr. Wonderful and . . . whoever else might be lurking out there out of our minds."

"How can Brooks pretend that I don't exist?" Faith pleaded. "Does he hate me that much? I've tried to call him seven times now. Seven! The guy who lives down the hall from him must think I'm a maniac. Brooks refuses to call me back."

KC reached out and touched her arm. "Give him time."

"Let's think about something else." Winnie twisted her earrings. "Look at the sky. The clouds."

"I don't hate Brooks," Faith ranted. "I just wanted my life to change, and now I feel like he's pretending I never existed. And that just makes me feel guilty, like I did something wrong and terrible. But I didn't. I didn't! He'll never understand."

"The grass," Winnie continued. "The bugs in the grass. The trash cans. The trash in the trash cans."

"If Brooks doesn't want to talk to me anymore,"

Faith decided, "then I have to pretend he doesn't exist, either."

Winnie kept on blabbing. She could tell that Faith was on the verge of tears. "Look at those soccer players, but don't see Brooks. Just see . . . um, feet and socks and scuzzy T-shirts." She paused. "You'd think they could at least have uniforms."

"What?"

"I mean, they *are* the official dorm league. I, as a dorm dweller, would like my team to have a decent uniform." Winnie slapped her forehead. "I'm babbling, I know it. But at least this babble is for a good cause. For my friends."

"Friends," Faith repeated, as if it were a vow.

"Friends," KC said, as if by rote. Suddenly her entire body straightened, like she'd been jolted by lightning. "Oh, God. Oh, yes! That's it!"

"What?"

KC spun around and grabbed Winnie with a fierce expression. "Winnie, you're brilliant."

"Tell it to my teachers."

Faith had her head down and was trudging on ahead, but KC hung back, clutching Winnie's arm and staring at her. "Win, you just gave me a fabulous idea."

"Like I said, what are friends for?"

"Yes. That's it! *Yes!*" KC threw her arms around Winnie, kissed her, then broke into a leap and a run.

Winnie shook her head. "And I have the reputation for being the crazy one of this trio."

But KC barely heard her. She was running again, almost skipping, no longer out of breath. When she caught up to Faith, she smiled broadly, then gave her a hug, too.

Faith sighed. "Thanks, KC. I needed that."

"Yeah," KC said, even though she was thinking about Steven Garth—and how she was going to dazzle him with her project idea.

Five

....

"I won't have you back in my life, Dennison. I won't."

"You have no choice, Amanda. When you kidnapped that baby, you dragged me back into your life. And like it or not, I'm staying here."

"You're not! I don't care what you say. I'll fight. I'll run. I'll do whatever I have to do to get away from you."

"Including kill?"

Amanda glared at Dennison through heavy-lidded eyes. Her nostrils flared. "Yes. If it comes to that. If I have to, I'll kill."

Dennison turned away and the goopy music swelled. It was quickly replaced by a happy-go-lucky jingle for microwave Pop Tarts.

"So much for today's episode of 'The Best and the Beloved,' " Lauren said out loud as she switched off her TV.

She was answered by the sound of someone practicing a flute downstairs and muffled conversation in Kimberly's dorm room next door. Lauren sat on the edge of her desk chair, facing the flat, gray screen. Alone.

Apparently Faith, Winnie, and KC had forgotten about their daily meeting to watch the soap opera. Not that they'd missed much. From what Lauren had gathered, the scene between Amanda and Dennison would be repeated in a different form every day that week, so they really only had to watch one episode a week to keep abreast of the story.

Of course, the reason they'd wanted to watch the dumb soap together every day hadn't been to keep tabs on "The Best and the Beloved" 's story lines. The reason—or at least Lauren had hoped it was the reason—was for all of them to be together.

Lauren put her hands to her soft, round face. She felt the ache of lonely tears. Hoping to distract herself, she took out her contacts, replacing them with round, wire-rimmed glasses. Then she took off her drab cardigan sweater and pulled on the old nightshirt that was hanging over the back of her chair. She leaned back to check herself in the full-length mirror.

"I look like some poor novelist living in a garret,"

she decided proudly. She wondered what her mother or the Tri Betas would say if they saw her.

Lauren also wondered if KC had really forgotten the soap opera, or if her desertion was intentional. Maybe KC had talked Faith and Winnie into keeping their distance, too. Lauren couldn't blame them. What did she have to offer, anyway? The use of her car. Her credit card. A dinner out. A big contribution to the sorority fund. She wondered what would happen if all that suddenly disappeared. The Tri Betas certainly wouldn't want her. Maybe KC, Faith, and Winnie felt exactly the same way.

"Stop feeling sorry for yourself," Lauren said out loud. She laid her cheek next to her computer keyboard on the old desk, kicked off her loafers, and hugged her thick middle. "At least you can take people to dinner and drive a great car." Then she cringed and thought about her mother.

"I knew you would never feel comfortable in those dreary dorms," her mother had said just before she'd left. "Why you ever picked this school in the first place, I will never know. The only thing worthwhile here is the sorority, and you certainly don't seem very excited about that. I don't know why you don't just pack up your things again and leave."

Lauren hadn't admitted that part of the University of Springfield's attraction was that her mother hated it. Of course, her mother wouldn't have understood that reasoning, just like she wouldn't understand how important it was that Lauren stick with U of S. After moving every two years when she was growing up, Lauren felt that if she didn't invest in something long-range, something *real,* at least once in her life, she would go completely nuts.

But what was real? Getting made over by Marielle? Learning secret sorority handshakes and taking part in sing-alongs? Lauren had hoped it might include becoming friends with Faith and Winnie—and KC. But she was beginning to think that she was just a useless, unwanted fourth.

Lauren switched on her computer and ran her short fingers across the keys. After bringing up her word-processing program, she typed in *help.*

Then she cleared the screen and quickly brought up the first piece she was working on for her writing class. The assignment was to describe something from her childhood, and Lauren had finished it in the middle of the previous night, working on a burst of inspiration while Faith slept.

She'd described an old swing set out behind the house on Long Island where they'd lived when she was nine. As she read her piece over, big tears rolled down her cheeks with the recollection. It all came back: the motion of the swing, the way the roses had made the air smell musty and sweet, the mangy span-iel who'd chased the swing, running back and forth under the jungle gym and barking, the lonely vastness of her parents' house.

Over and over Lauren read her short piece, noting the bitter remembrance as well as the sweet. She was a talented writer. It was the one positive thing she knew about herself. Not only had she been accepted to U of S's prominent writing program—an unusual achievement for a freshman—but she felt her ability under her well-padded, protective skin.

Quickly Lauren printed out a copy of her story, grabbed it just as it fed out of the printer, and read it again. She got up and began to pace. Back and forth she went. There was an idea sticking in the back of Lauren's mind, but she didn't have the nerve to let it all the way out.

And that was when it caught her eye. A copy of the college newspaper lying on Faith's desk. A destination. A chance. A slight possibility that someone, somewhere might be able to see beyond the Lauren her parents had created into the Lauren who existed now.

Lauren took off her nightshirt and put her sweater back on. She discarded her glasses and replaced them with her lenses again. She ran a comb through her fluffy hair, stuck her story in her expensive leather pouch, found her Mont Blanc fountain pen, and went out to look for her future.

Fifteen minutes later, she was in the dingy office of *The U of S Weekly Journal*.

"You want to place a classified, just fill out a card," said the young man behind the desk.

"Excuse me, but I don't want to place an ad," Lauren said.

"You want a subscription?" He laughed. "You don't need one. *The Weekly Journal* is free. Free to the students. Free to the people." He didn't look up. "Unless you're not a student, that is. Or a person. Then you gotta pay."

The Journal's office was in the basement floor of Beckman Hall, the journalism building. It was a vast, badly-lit room cluttered with desks and computers, stacks of newspapers, paste-up boards, bookshelves, droopy plants, dirty coffee cups, messy stacks, files, cards, photographs, a few moth-eaten sweaters, and a Cabbage-Patch doll with electrical tape over its mouth. In spite of all the odd personal mementos, only one human was there.

"I'm a student," Lauren informed him politely. "A freshman."

He was engrossed in the stack of articles he was going over. Carefully he read the first page of each, then skimmed the rest before tossing it onto a messy pile on the floor. "Good for you."

"I have a piece of writing I would like the editor to read."

"Don't we all," he muttered.

Lauren hugged her leather pouch against her thigh and fretted. She'd barely gathered the nerve to go in there, and wasn't sure what to do next.

He was no help. A placard on the desk announced his name was Dash Ramirez, assistant editor. His eyes were dark, and he had longish, wavy black hair, carelessly held back with a red bandanna. His T-shirt had once been blue . . . or green. Now it was mottled and ink-stained.

"I'm interested in writing for the newspaper. I stopped by to drop off a sample of my writing and to get some information. Can you help me? Please."

Dash Ramirez sighed, as if Lauren were a huge annoyance he hoped would go away. A cigarette burned in the ashtray next to him, and before answering her he stuck the butt in the corner of his mouth. "Who've you written for before?" He squinted as a stream of cigarette smoke drifted past his left eye.

The pattern of his speech was so musical and clipped that even Lauren recognized it as Latino. She listened to her own voice peep out, delicate as fine china. "I did an arts column for my prep-school paper in New York, and when I was in boarding school in Switzerland I did articles on what was happening here in America." As soon as she'd said it, she wished she could take the words back.

"La-di-da," Dash muttered, going over his papers

again and holding the cigarette, which was burning so low Lauren knew it would singe his fingers.

"Careful," she warned.

"Huh?"

"Your cig—"

"Jeez!" He shook his hand free of the cigarette, then looked up as if the burn had been all her fault. "So what do you want to do for us? Lifestyles of the rich and famous?"

"No."

Dash blew on his burned finger, and held out his palm—also ink-stained—in request of her story. She balanced the paper on his palm. Immediately he let it slide onto the top of his pile. Then he skimmed over it in record time. A few seconds later, her paper joined the mess under the table.

"Did you really read it?" she asked, amazed at her sudden burst of anger. She'd worked on that piece for seven hours. He hadn't spent more than seven seconds looking at it.

"I read enough. I can usually tell by the first sentence." Dash shrugged. "It's okay. You've got some talent. But it's a mood piece. What can you do for us? This isn't some polite literary magazine, or a social gazette."

"You could let me try something. You certainly wouldn't have to print it. If it's too awful you don't even have to show it to your editor."

"Don't worry, I wouldn't."

"Just give me a chance. Give me an assignment. A tryout piece. I'll write about anything."

Dash exhaled heavily. Then he checked his desk clock and shrugged. "Okay," he said as if he had nothing to lose, "you want an assignment, I'll give you one. One that's commensurate with your experience, and if you don't know what the word *commensurate* means, I suggest you look it up in the dictionary."

"I know what it means."

"Yeah. Okay," Dash repeated. "Here it is. We'll be putting out a supplement with the homecoming issue, so we'll need extra pieces. Filler stuff. Light junk for the old-timers to read when they come back for the big game, to make them feel all weepy and nostalgic." He searched under papers and empty yogurt containers, finally finding a printed list. "Let's see. Here's one for you. You live in the dorms?"

Lauren nodded.

"Dorm life."

"What?"

"Dorm life. That's your topic. Give me three hundred words. Typed. Double-spaced. No globs of whiteout bigger than a cockroach. I want it a week from Friday. Any later and you might as well throw it in the trash. It's just a tryout piece, to see what you come up with. And if you can make a deadline."

"Dorm life?" Lauren cringed. Dorm life sounded like the dreckiest, most tired, hackneyed title for an article she'd ever heard. What was she supposed to write about? The dining commons? Meeting your roommate? The way people decorated their rooms? "Isn't there anything else? Any other topic I could try for the supplement?"

Dash scooted back from his desk. He began picking up some other articles that had been submitted and shaking his head. It was as if Lauren had already left the office.

"Guess not," she mumbled. "I'm sorry. Dorm life is just fine."

When Dash didn't lift his head, she began to shuffle out. "Dorm life," she mouthed. She'd have to come up with some kind of angle, something to make it different and interesting.

Just as Lauren was reaching for the door, she heard Dash call out, "You're welcome."

Lauren glanced back at him, but he was involved in his papers again.

Six

By Thursday, KC was really prepared.

"Did we all come up with a brilliant idea?" Steven asked, his eyes glued to KC. They had broken into their business teams again and that smug smile was all over his face.

KC gestured for Helen and Edward to go first so they could get their presentations over with and give her their full attention. KC was confident. Since her flash of inspiration after the jog with Faith and Winnie, she'd spent every free moment gathering facts. She'd been to the dustiest stacks in the library and worked out drawings and graphs. She'd even gone behind Faith's back to consult with Brooks. She'd borrowed Lauren's BMW to do research downtown and was so ready she could have made a pitch before the entire lecture class.

Helen sighed, then admitted she hadn't thought of a single idea. "But I do like the concept," she offered. "If someone else has a good notion, I'll sure help."

KC hadn't expected much more, and Steven sluffed it off. Next, Edward presented a confusing suggestion about a typing service.

"Typing?" KC was skeptical.

"Doesn't sound too appealing to me, either." Steven shrugged. He patted Edward's shoulder.

Then KC and Steven glared at each other as the sun poured in and the wall clock gave its ponderous tick.

"After you," he challenged.

"Oh, no. After you," KC insisted.

Steven balanced on the desktop again, one bare foot popping in and out of a scuffed loafer. He was wearing a designer oxford-cloth shirt that he hadn't bothered to iron. His khakis were creased, too, though they were clearly the best khakis money could buy.

"Personalized license plate frames," Steven said. "I know where to get them. Ones that say University of Springfield. That way you don't have to put a sticker on your back window, but you can still let everybody on the road know that you made it into college."

"And we know how much you like to communicate with other people on the road," KC couldn't resist pointing out. "But I'm amazed you even notice something as mundane as a license plate in that Batmobile you drive."

"I wouldn't exactly call your Beamer the starving-student special."

KC froze for a moment. Of course. How could he have known she was driving someone else's car?

Helen and Edward were staring, so Steven got back on track. "Okay, little angel. Let's hear your idea. Blow us away. What do you have that's better?"

KC was beginning to worry that no matter how brilliant a venture she dreamed up, Steven would never let her win. She lifted up her briefcase, unsnapped the button, and pulled out her materials. "Soccer shirts."

"What?" Edward squinted.

"Soccer shirts?" repeated Helen.

Steven slid down off the desktop and landed—*plunk*—in the chair. Arms folded and legs outstretched, he leaned back in a prove-it recline.

KC plunged ahead. "A hundred and twenty freshmen in the dorms have signed up for an intramural soccer league. They start competing in another month, and from what I found out, they don't have uniforms."

Steven sat poker-faced.

"The guy who's running the whole thing is an old high-school friend of mine and I talked to him about it. He didn't think they'd fork over for socks and shorts, but he was positive they'd want jerseys. Especially if we could get ones with the players' names on them."

Edward nodded. Helen smiled. Steven was still flipping that loafer, lounging like he was on the beach at Waikiki.

KC turned her fact sheet to the other side. "I found a place in downtown Springfield that makes athletic shirts." She presented a brochure from Bernhard's Wholesale Athletic Supplies. "We'd let different teams choose their own style and colors. Bernhard's can get custom shirts to us in a few weeks. We can probably mark up each one a few dollars. Then we can share the profit among the four of us."

Edward was grinning. "Good. Soccer," he said, getting excited so that his English became even more awkward. "Very good. Soccer. Very good."

Helen smiled. "Yes, it is a good idea."

But Steven still seemed unmoved and unimpressed. His mocking smile hadn't reappeared, but KC worried that he was merely resting, gathering energy for a more aggressive attack.

She forged ahead. "I know you think your license plate–frame idea is better, but this will be a one-time business, which is perfect for our class assignment.

We get people interested in the shirts, take the orders, collect the money, order from Bernhard's, deliver the shirts, and we're done. Then we can analyze how we did, what we learned, how much money we made. It's perfect for this class.''

"Soccer shirts," Steven pondered.

"Yes! It's a good idea and you know it. I don't care how hard you try to fight me and put me down, you have to admit it's the best idea!"

"Okay, Angeletti. It's the best idea. Now what?"

"What do you mean, now what?"

Steven dragged himself back up to a sitting position. He perched his face on his fists and dared KC with his eyes. "Soccer shirts okay with you two?" he asked Edward and Helen, not taking his gaze off KC.

Helen nodded while Edward almost jumped in his chair.

Suddenly Steven pitched forward in his chair as if he were about to go into orbit. He held up one finger. "First point, Angeletti: Did you get any sample shirts for us to see?"

KC stammered.

Steven flicked the brochure back to her. He counted off his second point on his fingers. "You're going to need more than that black-and-white brochure to sell those shirts, you know. Did you find out if they have a minimum order?"

"No . . ."

"Did you open a business bank account, get to know someone at the bank?"

"No," KC mumbled. "But I will. I will!"

"We'll need to go downtown and buy some sample shirts, so people can get a real idea of what they're ordering. I'll do that. Edward, why don't you do some flyers? Can you handle that? And Helen, you drive, don't you?"

Helen nodded.

"How about being in charge of pick-up and delivery?"

"All right."

KC wanted to strangle Steven. Instead of trashing her idea, he was taking it over! "And what am I supposed to do?" she rebelled. "Take notes and answer your telephone?"

Steven grinned and stared at KC again. "If you want. Actually, I thought you could go downtown with me to pick out the samples."

"I don't want to go anywhere with you."

Steven was unfazed. "So meet me down there. Monday. Noon."

Before KC could think up another comeback, Steven had his wallet open and was taking out a twenty-dollar bill.

He slapped it on the table. "Okay. We need some capital to invest. We'll have to pay for the sample shirts. Fork over whatever you can afford and you'll be repaid out of the profits.''

Helen and Edward didn't hesitate. They were both so carried away by Steven's energy that Edward counted out twelve dollars in ones while Helen pulled a fresh ten out of a tiny leather change purse.

Suddenly they were all staring at KC. It took her a moment to realize that they were waiting for her to contribute, too. But despite her silk blouse—which she'd worked all summer to buy—and her briefcase (a graduation present), there wasn't more than a dollar and change in her purse. She took up the clothing brochure again and pretended to be absorbed in it.

Steven gathered up the cash, gesturing for Edward to keep a record of the amounts. "Put your money where your mouth is, little angel. Think you could spare a little gas money from your BMW?"

KC's neck went rigid as it finally hit her. Steven assumed that she was as spoiled and well off as he was.

"I'm sorry," she stammered, scribbling on the corner of her fact sheet. "I don't have any cash on me. I don't usually carry any."

Steven laughed. "Who are you? Prince Charles or something?"

KC gave him a mysterious smile. At least she hoped it looked mysterious.

By then Naomi, who was making her rounds, was waiting to check in with their team and find out what they were cooking up. Of course Steven shot up before KC could stop him. No longer lounging like a languid beach bum, he was talking in the TA's face so fast that KC thought she could see Naomi's eyes whirl.

When Steven sat back down, he slid in his chair and drummed the desktop, gloating. "Naomi loves it. We're in."

KC cringed as Steven slapped Edward's palms. When it was her turn, he put out his hand, then pulled it back and laughed. He took in every inch of her face.

"See you on Monday," he dared. "Don't be late."

KC glared back. Like it or not, she and Steven Garth weren't just classmates anymore. They were partners.

"I've got to stop eating this," Winnie groaned that evening. She began doing leg lifts on the dorm-room floor while stretching her arm to put back her half-eaten slice of deluxe pineapple-bacon pizza.

All four of them were together, crammed into Faith and Lauren's room, which was also littered with Faith's theater magazines, KC's spreadsheets, Lauren's computer, CD player, and microwave, and three partially eaten pizzas—Lauren's treat.

"Why not scarf it down?" KC asked. She sat on Faith's bed, adding up figures on a calculator she'd borrowed from Lauren. Since she'd thought up the soccer-shirt venture the day before, she'd been acting like a possessed accountant. Her fingers zapped around the tiny keys like fireflies. "Didn't you run today?"

"Only thirty laps," Winnie said. She threw her legs over her head in a yoga stretch, pulling her knees so close to her ears that she could feel her vertebrae being pulled apart. "I'm into moderation."

Faith, who was at her desk flipping through another *Theatercrafts,* exchanged glances with KC. They both laughed.

Lauren was trying to share the joke between Faith and KC. She turned away from her computer screen with a tentative smile.

"Actually, I was going to skip dinner." Winnie pinched herself, feeling for any extra flesh on her thighs. "But then I probably would have just roamed the halls later, looking for stray cookie crumbs and cans of Coke."

They all groaned.

"And run the risk of bumping into Josh." Winnie uncurled and tugged on Lauren's tweed pant leg. "So, thanks for saving me from myself."

Lauren whispered, "Anytime."

A strange silence among them followed. The tree outside Faith and Lauren's window scratched the glass and someone in the dorm turned up opera music on their stereo. Winnie sensed that Lauren had forked over for the pizzas so that she wouldn't have to be alone. That seemed strange to Winnie, who would never have thought of securing her friends' company with a few rounds of dough, some greasy cheese, and pineapple chunks. But that evening Winnie hadn't wanted to be alone, either. And as much as she was beginning to admire Melissa, she could only stare at the back of Melissa's red head for so long while Melissa did her biology homework.

Winnie knew she should have stayed home and studied, too, but she still hadn't decided on two new classes to replace the ones she'd dropped. She was beginning to feel as if she were carrying a load of cement on her back.

Even worse, since she'd dropped those classes she'd had too much extra space in her brain: too much room to fill with thoughts of Josh, too much time to regret her mistake of pushing the romance too fast, and to wonder each time she went out her dorm-room door if she would run into him.

Faith looked up from her magazine. "Did you guys hear about Lauren and the newspaper?"

Winnie shook her head. It was almost as if Faith were a nursery-school teacher saying, *Now kids, I think Lauren is feeling a little left out. Let's all make an effort to include her.* "No. What?"

Lauren typed in something on her keyboard. She'd

been to some sorority decorating party that afternoon and still wore her wool pants and lace-collared sweater. "I'm just writing a tryout article on life in the dorms. I thought I'd interview people who live in different halls. Maybe throw pizza parties like this, so people will want to come and talk to me. I need to find an interesting angle."

Winnie considered saying, *I don't really think you'll have to supply the entire dorm complex with pizza just to have them talk to you.* But she realized she'd do the same thing just to have Josh come and talk to her. "I'll give you an interesting angle," she said. "How about what not to do your first week in the dorms?"

Lauren wrinkled her nose.

"Just kidding." Winnie did a full-body stretch and then leaped to her feet. "Speaking of dorm life, I saw Brooks at lunch today."

KC stopped punching numbers into her calculator and Faith froze.

"I asked him if he was ever going to talk to you again, Faith. He practically pretended that he didn't remember who you were." KC was giving her a "drop it" stare, while Faith had resumed frantically flipping magazine pages. "Sorry. I shouldn't have mentioned it."

Soon Lauren was staring at her computer screen again and Faith was tearing out an article from her magazine while KC calculated and calculated. Winnie hadn't come over to be silent and watch over people do their homework—she could do that back in her own room with Melissa. So she took a slice of plain pizza, trotted around the room giving each of her friends a kiss on the head, and said goodbye.

Quickly, Winnie jogged downstairs, pumping her knees high for extra calorie burn-up while holding the pizza above her head. Some people were gathered around the Rapids Hall lobby piano singing show tunes, but as soon as Winnie jogged out across the green, it was quiet again.

The peaceful night lasted until she got close to her own dorm. Noise blasted out of Forest Hall. Unlike the cabaret atmosphere of the Rapids Hall lobby or the morgue-like quiet of KC's study dorm, the lobby of Forest Hall had not gone two straight nights without a monster party. Winnie heard the heavy-metal music and the screeching laughter, saw the limbs swaying like palm trees in a storm as couples boogied and groped.

"No, thanks," she said to herself, avoiding the most direct route to her room, which was through the lobby and straight down the hall. "I think I'll be a party pooper for this one night at least." She went the long way around, up through the basement. She hurried past the *clunk* of the soda machines and the *ping* of video games until she was back on the first floor. The bass from the lobby stereo shook the thin cream-colored walls.

Winnie hurried past Josh's closed door and opened her own. Melissa was in bed, slowly turning pages in a fat, hardbound textbook. When Winnie entered, Melissa looked up and offered a tolerant smile.

Winnie closed the door. The lobby ruckus was reduced to rhythmic vibrations and occasional muffled screams.

"I brought you some pizza," Winnie said. She was relieved to have made a peace treaty with Melissa. But it was still nothing like coming home to a close friend.

"Thanks." Melissa read one last paragraph. "But I don't eat pizza. Not when I'm in training."

"Oh." Winnie shrugged and dropped the slice in her trash can. "Right."

Melissa yawned, took off her glasses, and bent back the corner of her page. "By the way, there was a letter for you in our mailbox. It must be from someone on campus, because there's no stamp on it. I put it on your bed."

"Thanks."

Melissa closed her book, turned off her lamp, and, for all Winnie could tell, fell soundly and immediately asleep.

Meanwhile, Winnie's heart had skipped a beat. She shed her kimono, scarves, bracelets, earrings, and socks, remembering to stow each article in a drawer or at least toss it on the bottom of her closet rather than leaving a trail across the floor. Then she picked up the envelope and held it against her bare skin.

It *was* a letter from someone on campus. No stamp. No address, really. Just Winnie's name and room number scribbled in pencil.

Winnie knew what it had to be. At last. Josh. It was a letter from Josh. She could already imagine what it said.

Win—
What a mess. Let's talk. Now. Soon. I miss you like crazy and you seem to think that I don't want to see you anymore. Let's clear things up ASAP. I love . . .

Winnie was already close to tears, feeling warm and wonderful and totally confused, when she tore open the envelope.

It said:

Winifred Lynn Gottlieb:
It has come to our attention that you have dropped two classes. Any freshman carrying less than ten credit hours must discuss his or her academic situation with a counselor. You have an

appointment next Monday at 9:00 with Mr. Morain in Administration Hall, room 247. Please call if you need to reschedule.

The warmth and wonder had turned to a big, empty blank. All Winnie wanted was to forget about everything and go to sleep.

Seven

The campus branch of Western Interstate Bank was decorated with huge photographs that hung down from the ceiling: snow-capped mountains, skiers racing downhill in tight crouches, Mill Pond on a sunny day with a family of ducks in the foreground and canoes crisscrossing behind.

KC sat under those photographs in a padded vinyl chair. Brooks was next to her, and they both could see it was going to be a long wait. The place was bustling. It seemed that every other U of S student had picked that Friday afternoon to open an account or check on a student loan.

"Thanks for helping me with this," KC said.

"Hmm?" Brooks replied vaguely. He hunched forward with his hands clasped. In some ways he was exactly the same Brooks KC had known since junior high. His tan was even. His hair curled down the back of his neck and over his ears. He wore neat pleated trousers with a red hiking parka.

One thing wasn't familiar about Brooks. The Brooks KC had known had always been sure. He'd always seemed to know what he wanted and how he was going to get it. But that was before the breakup. Now he seemed preoccupied and spacey.

"Oh, I don't mind helping you," he said. "Anything for an old friend. I've been trying to keep myself really busy all week."

KC craned her neck to check the bank officers' desks. It was after two-thirty. She prayed that they would get to her before closing time. "Keeping busy shouldn't have been hard, with the first week of classes and all."

He nodded slowly, as if his head had grown very heavy. "Yeah. And I've been trying to get into everything that's going on with my dorm. That's why I took charge of the whole intramural soccer thing." He reached in his pocket and pulled out some folded pages. "Oh, by the way, here's the player roster you wanted. The name of every player who signed up is on there. I rewrote it for you, arranged it by dorm team, and put down everybody's room number."

KC took the roster as carefully as if it had been a

stock certificate for a thousand shares. As she'd expected, Brooks had given her a clearly typed list. "Thank you so much." She noticed Brooks check his watch, an underwater model with lots of buttons and dials. "That's all I needed, Brooks. You don't have to wait with me if you don't want to. This may take a while."

"Really. Everybody's in here getting spending money for their hot weekend dates." He leaned back, stared at the hanging photographs, and let out a long, painful huff.

"Brooks."

"I still can't believe it happened," he suddenly raved. "I don't understand. KC, you're one of her best friends. Did you see it coming? Did Faith tell you she was going to break up with me? I was totally unprepared. Totally." He ran a hand through his curls and sat up again. "Sorry. You don't want to hear this."

Actually, part of KC did want to hear it. Despite her supposed immunity to men, she was intensely curious about what made guys tick. And somehow the irritation of Steven Garth had just made her more curious. She usually accused Winnie of being a flake because she went through so many boyfriends. And sometimes she thought of Faith as a chicken, since— until now—Faith had stuck with the first guy she'd ever dated. But sometimes KC suspected that both Winnie and Faith were braver than she.

"I just keep thinking that something must have happened. Something definite," Brooks decided. "Maybe she met some other guy." He waited, as if to see whether or not KC would confirm his suspicion.

KC didn't move. Flashes of Christopher Hammond went on and off in her brain. She hoped that she hadn't given anything away. And yet she could feel Brooks move closer.

"Is there somebody else? Is that it? KC, you've got to tell me."

KC tried to wipe any expression off her face. "Why don't you talk to Faith about it?" she answered. "It's so weird how you won't talk to Faith, and now Faith won't talk to you! But you both tell me what's going on, which is even weirder."

Brooks swung in his chair so that he was facing her. "So there *is* somebody else?" he said. "What did Faith tell you?"

KC knew that whatever feelings Faith had for Christopher, they were none of Brooks's business—and probably had had nothing to do with the breakup anyway. Even Faith had admitted that it was all fantasy with Christopher. And yet KC sensed that Brooks had latched onto the subject of his rival and was going to stick with it. She remembered how in high school

Brooks had found out that someone had stuffed the ballot box for a school election. He wouldn't let it go until the cheater had been found out and put out of office. Brooks had that same stubborn, tenacious expression now.

KC was relieved when a fiftyish woman in a pink suit with a sprayed, bubble hairdo looked right at her and asked if she was next. KC nodded.

"It's my turn. Thanks again, Brooks," KC said, getting up. "I'll see you later."

As soon as KC sat down at the desk with the bank officer, she tried to forget about Brooks and remember what an important encounter this was. She had to make a good impression. Steven Garth was waiting for her to make a mistake so he could rub it in.

"I'm Pamela Myers," the bank officer said. She had a maternal manner and wore clunky lavender jewelry. "What can I do for you?"

"I'm Kahia Angeletti," KC said, clearing her throat as she introduced herself.

"What a distinctive name," Ms. Myers said.

KC cringed. She considered the name her parents had dumped on her a lifetime label of flakiness. "I'd like to open a bank account. I already have a personal account at the Ben Franklin Bank, off campus. But this is for a business we're starting. It's for a class."

Ms. Myers lifted one penciled-in eyebrow. "What is your business called?"

KC had to think fast as she pulled out the cash that Steven, Edward, and Helen had contributed in class. "Oh . . . Soccer, Inc. That's our name. Soccer, Inc. I'd like to open the account with this."

Ms. Myers pulled cards out from her drawer, then stuck them in her typewriter. "What kind of a business is this? It sounds like an interesting assignment."

KC explained all about their endeavor: how it wasn't really the assignment, but that they'd decided to be creative and do something other than a mundane book report. Actually, KC got carried away talking about Soccer, Inc. She was beginning to worry that she was babbling like Winnie, but Ms. Myers kept smiling and nodding.

Ms. Myers handed KC four signature cards. "You and your partners should each sign one of these, since it's a joint account. Would you like *Soccer, Inc.* printed on the checks?"

"Yes. Thank you." KC stowed the cards while the bank officer wrote out a receipt.

"I must say that I admire your initiative. I think it's marvelous. Are you a freshman?"

KC nodded.

Ms. Myers plucked a colorful folder off her desk. "Why don't you fill this out, too, while you're here? It's a special credit card our bank is offering for promising new students. The charge limit is two hundred dollars."

KC stared at the application, which had a photo of the Western Charge Card on the front, a sparkly orange rectangle with a picture of bucking broncos. Her parents didn't believe in credit cards. They always said that the only people who benefited from plastic were the credit-card companies. It was just that attitude that made KC suspect that a credit card was about the best thing she could have right then. "Really?"

"I can issue you a temporary card today," Ms. Myers said. "Just fill out the application and I'll make up a card for you."

KC filled in the information, then waited while Ms. Myers took the soccer deposit and the application up to a teller window. A few minutes later she returned, placing a shiny orange rectangle in front of KC. "You can make your payments through the mail or right here in the bank, whichever is more convenient. Congratulations."

KC stared at the card. *Kahia Cayanne Angeletti* was stamped across it, but KC felt that for the first time in her life she could look at that name and feel proud. She picked up the rectangle of stiff plastic and put it in her wallet. "Thank you. Thank you so much."

Ms. Myers stood up and shook her hand. "It's lovely to meet you, Kahia. If there's anything else I can help you with, please let me know."

* * *

"What is your impression so far of dorm life?"

"My room reminds me of a cell at Alcatraz."

"My dorm reminds me of Camp Minnitukka. I'm half expecting the other girls on my floor to sing 'Rise and Shine.' "

"I'm going to start keeping a count on my wall, marking off the days until I can move out at the end of freshman year."

"What do you mean? Don't you like getting woken up by some guy who gargles so loudly you can hear it through your floor?"

"And what about the food?"

"Blech!"

Giggles, slaps, moans, and little hugs.

Lauren knew that her interviewees were goofing around, but she couldn't blame them. After Lauren stupidly had mentioned her newspaper article to Marielle, her big sister had decided that the other Tri Beta pledges should be Lauren's first focus group. So Lauren was in the middle of the Tri Beta living room, surrounded by big, overstuffed sofas, bouquets of red roses, little lace pillows, and the other freshmen girls who'd been selected as future sisters of the Tri Beta sorority. Marielle stood in the doorway, shaking her charm bracelet and watching with a brittle smile.

"Thank you for your . . . interesting answers." Lauren took a deep breath and decided to try again.

"How do you feel about your roommates?"

"Mine bites her toenails."

"Thank God I only have to live with mine one year. I can't wait to move into this house when I'm a sophomore."

"Mine lets her boyfriend stay over—while I'm there."

"My boyfriend practically is my roommate."

"You guys think you have it bad! My roommate is pledging Kappa Kappa Gamma!"

That was followed by a huge "Boo" and "Cut down the Kappas," which was followed by throw-up noises until the pledges fell all over one another laughing. When they got up again they resumed their moussing and polishing, plucking, hemming, and brushing. It was Friday night, and they were all primping for a big party that night at the Omega Delta Tau house. The pledges would all be heading over later with their big sisters.

Lauren knew she should have held her first interviews at the dorms, but since she was required to be at the frat-party preparation session, she'd foolishly decided to take Marielle's advice and kill two birds with one stone.

"Just a few more questions," Lauren promised.

"Nooooooo!"

"Dorm life is too dreary to discuss."

There were groans, manicured hands covering

pretty faces, delicate shoulders turning away. Lauren felt her stomach clench as she thought back to Dash Ramirez and how he'd probably expected a scene like this. Maybe she was too timid ever to write about anything real or interesting. In desperation, Lauren picked up the decorated basket she'd filled with little thank-you presents—lipsticks and felt pens, barrettes and bottles of nail polish—and passed it around. Each girl picked out a gift, then looked back at Lauren with a more agreeable expression.

Lauren read over the rest of her questions. She'd hoped to get some real insight into how girls felt about some serious issues, such as coed living, lack of privacy, finding enough study time, being away from home. But she also knew that the sorority pledges wanted nothing more than to prove to Marielle that dorm life sucked in comparison with their glittering futures as Tri Betas.

"Thank you," Lauren said to the group. "I've got everything I need. You've all been a big help."

There was a sigh of relief as Lauren got up. Marielle joined her immediately. Lauren's big sister had helped herself to a tube of lipstick and was testing it on the back of her hand.

"Did you get good interviews?" Marielle asked.

Lauren stared at the floor.

"I knew you would. Now sit down again, because you and I have important things to do."

Lauren obeyed, her plump legs folding beneath her. "Pull back your hair and let me really look at you."

Lauren did as Marielle requested, then sat for another half-hour while Marielle blended and dabbed, giving her a makeover. When Lauren finally looked in the mirror, she saw her hair slicked down with gooey mousse, her eyes ringed and sunken, her mouth as red and shiny as Marielle's. She looked like a sick baby who'd just devoured red Jell-o.

"Thank you, Marielle," Lauren said.

Marielle shook her straight hair, letting it fall in a perfect slant over one eye. "It's a start," she said. "I wish I could loan you some clothes, but of course nothing of mine will fit you. Well, we'll see what we can do about that, too. But as far as the frat party tonight goes, I think we've made an improvement."

"Well, actually," Lauren mumbled, "I think I have to skip the party tonight. I have a terrible stomachache all of a sudden. I guess I'd better go back to the dorm."

KC was just outside the Tri Beta house, on the corner of Sorority Row. Brooks was still with her. He'd waited for her outside the bank. And no matter how she tried to shake him off and drop the subject of Christopher, Brooks was hanging on.

"So tell me about this Christopher Hammond," he wanted to know.

"Brooks, I told you, she's just working with him on his musical."

KC was beginning to understand why Faith might have broken up with Brooks. When he was determined to do something, Brooks was like a bulldog. KC wondered if the only way to get off the topic might be to wait until Brooks was looking in the other direction and run away.

But where was she going to run? Into the open front door of the Tri Beta house? KC needed to get to Zappy's Copy Center and make copies of the soccer roster. And to get to Zappy's she had to go right down Sorority Row.

"There's nothing between Faith and Christopher!" KC insisted. But Brooks didn't believe her.

If KC hadn't been so nerve-wrackingly close to the Tri Beta house, she never would have let the name of Christopher Hammond slip out. But this was the one street in Springfield where KC was an easy mark.

It had happened as soon as KC and Brooks had turned the corner and KC had seen that two-story white sorority house again. The sight of it wrung out her insides. The pots of pink mums out in front, the widow's walk on top, the front door open so that she could see the pledges gathered inside.

And if that hadn't been enough, just as KC was getting herself under control Courtney Conner had come out on the porch for a breath of fresh air. In a loden-green skirt and ribbon-trimmed jacket, Courtney stood taking deep, healthful breaths. The memory was wrenching. Courtney, who had taken KC under her wing, put her faith in KC, and then been forced to cut her off after KC dumped drinks on Marielle.

And just then was when Brooks had said, "KC, you already admitted that Faith mentioned some guy. Just tell me what she said about him. You can leave out the guy's name."

Before KC could catch herself, she replied, "She just said that she likes the way Christopher Hammond directs the musical. It's not some big—" Then she'd stopped and stamped the ground, wanting to slug herself and hide under the sidewalk at the same time.

"Christopher Hammond!" Brooks had repeated. "Christopher Hammond!"

"I can't believe I said that."

"Barney, my roommate, was thinking of pledging the Omega Delta Tau fraternity during orientation," Brooks had recalled. "I went with Barney to a frat interview at ODT. I met Christopher Hammond! He's a junior. A big deal!"

Before KC could stop him, Brooks had taken off in search of the ODT house. There was no stopping him, and all KC could do was hope that Courtney didn't see her as she hurried along and tried to catch up.

"Brooks!" she called out, wondering what he would do if he ran into Christopher.

But when they arrived at the ODT house, they both froze. KC knew instantly that Brooks wasn't going to do anything.

In front of the frat house was a new convertible with California plates and a Mills College sticker. A lovely girl was stepping out of it. Her hair reached down to her waist and was the color of Coca-Cola. She wore a pale-yellow dress that fluttered as she rose from the car and threw her arms around the neck of the young man who was obviously her boyfriend, obviously the beau she only got to see on occasional weekends. And even though she and her boyfriend were soon wound around each other in an ecstatic embrace, even though they were kissing, KC knew who the guy was. Christopher Hammond.

Eight

L auren's BMW was nimble and quick. The leather had a silky sheen and smelled like the world's finest shoe store.

"Is this a great car?" KC heaved.

Winnie gave a shrug and looked out the window. "It's okay. For a car."

It was Saturday. Lauren had lent KC the BMW, assuming that she was going downtown to look for a new job. Winnie had come along to get off campus for a while and pick up a book she hadn't been able to find at the university bookstore.

"I guess I'm not into cars." Winnie sat with her feet so high on the dashboard that they were practically dangling out the window. She took a classical

tape out of the player and replaced it with a cassette
of old Billie Holiday songs. "But maybe that's what
I should get interested in. Auto shop."

"Winnie, you can't be serious. I don't think they
teach auto shop in college, anyway. Why did you say
that?"

"No reason. Never mind."

"What about advertising?"

"What about it?"

"Remember all those campaigns you ran for me in
high school? You were great at it. What about ma-
joring in marketing or public affairs?"

"I don't know. I didn't do too well with my private affair. With Josh." Winnie blew a big pink bubble, then sucked it back into her mouth.

"That's not what I meant."

KC had been trying to peptalk Winnie all morning
and she was starting to run out of suggestions. *You've
got to do something besides mope over Josh and wonder why
you're not an achiever like Melissa!* she wanted to yell.
If there was one thing KC could do for her friends it
was to prod them, stimulate their ambition. Maybe
she wasn't always giving sympathy like Faith or material things like Lauren, but she gave nonetheless.
Her way of giving was to push the people she cared
about, to light a fire under them. But how could she
light a fire under someone who didn't want to be lit?

Winnie picked one of Lauren's paperbacks off the

seat and changed the subject. "I told Lauren I'd get some girls from my dorm together so she could talk to them. She seemed so bummed after trying to interview the Tri Beta pledges."

"I don't know why she's bothering to write about the dorms. She's a Tri Beta now, she should act like a Tri Beta."

Winnie put on a mock scowl. "And how does a Tri Beta act?"

KC stiffened.

"Why shouldn't Lauren write about the dorms?" Winnie went on. "That's the assignment she got. Sometimes I wish somebody would just give me an assignment. For my entire life. 'Winnie, sign up for anthropology and windsurfing. Eat yogurt and live to be a hundred. Winifred Lynn, walk right into Josh's room and tell him you're sick of thinking about him and you'd like to at least talk so that you can get him off your mind.' "

"Forget him," KC said.

"Easy for you to say. You've never had your mind invaded by some guy so that you can't think about anything else. It's like being taken over by an alien."

KC flinched and pulled over at Renton's Books, which was where Winnie wanted to go to pick up a book called *How to Organize Your Life—Starting with Your Closet*.

Winnie got out. "Thanks for the lift."

"Are you sure you don't want me to swing back by and pick you up?"

"No thanks. I'll jog. And I'll see you tonight for turkey à la king."

KC waved as Winnie ran into the store, then pulled back into traffic. Once again she let herself enjoy the responsiveness of Lauren's car. Compared to her father's ancient van, it was like commanding a jet plane. KC felt powerful behind the wheel. She wished that Steven would cruise around a downtown corner now.

But Steven and his Corvette were nowhere in sight. All KC saw was light Saturday downtown traffic: four-wheel-drive jeeps and pick-ups, station wagons, students on bicycles or behind the wheels of dinged-up compacts.

KC cruised through the traffic, weaving in and out of lanes, finally doubling back to The Strand, a few blocks of fancy shops in renovated eighteen-nineties brownstones. The idea of looking for a job was still with her, but she wanted to get Soccer, Inc. off the ground before she took on anything new. Besides, she had a brand-new credit card in her wallet, and there was no way KC was going to meet Mr. Batmobile on Monday, looking anything but business-like and totally spectacular.

There was a parking space at a meter right in the middle of The Strand. KC pulled up in front of an exclusive boutique called Frederika Shay. She knew her two hundred dollars of credit wouldn't go far in a shop like that, but maybe she could find a sale. She needed every advantage she could think of. If Steven wanted to assume that she was rich, that was his problem. She'd done nothing to mislead him, but she wasn't going to go out of her way to set him straight, either.

"May I help you?" a saleswoman asked as soon as KC stepped in. The shop was obviously expensive, but a little old-fashioned. No orange Day-Glo or fashion videos. Instead there were little antique sales desks and conservative suits hanging in wooden armoires. The store smelled of flowers and made KC think of the Tri Beta house.

KC spotted it right away, hanging on display between a huge Japanese vase and a table stacked with sweaters. It was a short and boxy jacket made of tightly-woven wool in forest green, with silver buttons in the shape of little acorns.

"I'd like to try that jacket on," KC said, trying not to sound intimidated.

A moment later she was wearing it. With her black pleated skirt, a lace blouse, and patent-leather flats, she knew it would look elegant and professional. It was perfect.

"It looks wonderful on you. And it's a terrific buy," the saleswoman said. She wore a chic but simple navy suit, the kind that never went out of style.

"Two hundred and twenty dollars, marked down from two-ninety-five."

KC's hopes fell flat. She wanted the jacket so much that her body ached for it. But her credit-card limit was two hundred dollars.

Unable to take the jacket off just yet, she fingered it and mumbled, "The button is coming off, and there's a little rip in the lining."

The saleswoman put her glasses on to confirm KC's observations. She clucked her tongue. "You're right. I'll mark it down to a hundred and ninety-five. How's that?"

KC hadn't mentioned the flaws in order to lower the price, although she realized that that should have been her intention. She also knew that Faith could repair those two flaws in about five seconds. "Oh, all right," she sighed, trying to contain her fabulous excitement. "I guess I'll take it."

"Fine."

Trying not to bounce off the walls and shriek with glee, KC met the saleswoman at her desk. She put down her new Western Charge. The woman examined the card, turning it over to check KC's signature.

"Is it all right?" KC couldn't help asking. For a moment she thought the saleswoman was going to throw the card back at her, say "Who are you trying to kid?" and chase her out of the shop.

The saleswoman smiled. "Of course. I just need to

call and get an authorization. It won't take me a minute.''

KC waited nervously while the woman made her call, reading the amount of the charge and the numbers of KC's card into the phone.

"Enjoy it," she said after hanging up and handing the sales slip over for KC to sign. A moment later the jacket was packed up in a silver-and-white bag.

"That's all?" It was hard for KC to believe that it could be so easy. She was flat broke, and yet she had been authorized to buy a jacket that cost almost two hundred dollars. The concept of credit was so delicious that KC could have kissed the saleswoman.

But of course, she didn't.. With great dignity, she took her package and said, "I will enjoy it. Thank you."

And then she walked out, feeling like the most successful, classiest, most beautiful college freshman on earth.

KC's euphoria didn't last long.

Forty minutes after buying the jacket, and just after slipping her last few quarters in the parking meter, she saw a pair of patent-leather flats in another Strand shop window. They were the exact pair of shoes she needed, the shoes she had to have or else the jacket wouldn't be worth having.

They were on sale, too. Forty-four ninety-five, marked down from seventy.

Even though KC knew that she couldn't buy them, she went in . . . just to look, to try them on, to hopefully find out that they didn't have her size, that they killed her feet, or that the shoes were really dreadful and ugly up close.

"A perfect fit," said the clerk.

"They are, aren't they?" KC moaned, wishing there was some way, any way, that she could buy them. Her feet glimmered like Dorothy's in *The Wizard of Oz*. Her mind raced. She could return the jacket and try to find a cheaper one. No. She could call her parents and see if they could spare some cash. But that would mean confessing that she'd lost her waitress job, which would mean explaining why she'd lost her job, which would also mean admitting that she'd tried to join a sorority. And since her parents thought the same of sororities as they did of credit cards, KC crossed that option off her list.

"Shall I wrap them up for you?" the clerk asked.

KC didn't respond. She was trying to figure out how to sneak out of the store when the clerk stuffed the shoes back in the box and, smiling at KC, took them to the sales counter.

KC joined him. Now she felt really stupid. It was like being at the Safeway when her mother was a few dollars short and they had to sort through the bran flakes, the veggie-burger mix, and the bean curd, deciding what to keep and what to put back.

She was too embarrassed to stop him as he went ahead, writing up the sale and asking, "Cash or charge?"

There certainly wasn't much cash in KC's pocket, so she handed over her charge card again. She knew that he would just call for an authorization and then tell her that he was sorry, she was over her limit. But to KC's amazement, the clerk didn't reach for the phone. He didn't even check the signature on the back of her card. He merely ran it through his little machine, handed the credit form over for her to sign, and said, "Thank you."

"Don't you have to call for an authorization?" KC breathed.

Just then a few more customers came in. As the clerk stuck KC's shoes and the receipt in a bag, he told her, "Only for purchases over fifty dollars. If it's under fifty, we don't have to bother."

"Thank you." KC hurried out of the shoe store as if she'd just learned how to shoplift. And yet she felt anything but dishonest. She was giddy with victory. She felt a lust, a shopping greed, a hunger to buy.

After that she slunk into a stationery store, where she bought a leather-covered date book. Again, she held her breath as she handed over her card, charging another forty dollars. But once again the clerk said nothing more than "Thank you" and "Come again." So KC kept shopping. She went from shop to shop to shop, buying all the things she absolutely had to have for the following week. She got stockings and a lacy scarf, gloves, perfume, and a fancy new calculator. She made sure that each purchase was under fifty dollars and racked it all up on her new Western Charge account.

"Can you bring up light number twelve, Merideth?"

"Sorry, Christopher, that's as bright as it goes."

"Faith? Faith, can you hear me up there?"

"I can hear you, Christopher."

"Can you find number twelve and point it more toward the center of the stage? That's it. You still okay up there?"

"I'm okay."

"Thanks. That looks a little brighter."

As far as Faith was concerned, the light in the nearly empty University Theater was blinding. No matter that the house lights were off. No matter that she was on a dark, perilous catwalk, suspended at least forty feet above the stage.

"Can't we get any more light on the front of the stage?" Christopher called. He was pacing in the house, up and down the left aisle.

Meanwhile, Merideth was on center stage directly beneath Faith, his curls looking very dark against a red flannel shirt and paisley suspenders. When he looked up at Faith, his glasses reflected the stage lights.

"Sorry," Merideth told Christopher. "We can't move any instruments because of *Hansel and Gretel.* We have to work with their set-up. It's going to stay like this."

"Welcome to college theater," Christopher muttered. He hopped up the temporary step unit that led over the orchestra pit and joined Merideth on the stage. "Faith, thanks. Why don't you come down?"

Gingerly, clutching the safety bars and inching along the walk, Faith made it back to the side wall. Then she took a deep breath and, not looking down, started down the wall ladder that led back to the stage floor. She dropped when she reached the last rung, sidestepping some sandbags and a heap of old velvet curtains. By the time she joined Christopher and Merideth, her legs were trembling and her breath was short.

Merideth stared as Faith shook her stinging palms. "You must have had a pretty impressive theater in your high school to be used to catwalks like that," he said with admiration.

Faith kept her gaze away from Christopher. "No. I've never been on a catwalk before."

"Why didn't you tell me that?" Merideth objected, whipping off his glasses in alarm. "I never would have let you climb up there if I'd known that."

Faith shrugged.

Merideth shook his head.

"Did I tell you this girl was something special?" Christopher took a step closer to Faith and gazed at her with even more appreciation. It looked like he'd had a haircut that morning, and he was wearing a starched white shirt, even though the theater was grungy.

Faith had on her OshKosh overalls and her hair was tied back in a French braid. "Thanks."

"And I told Merideth your idea about using abstract cubes for scenery. He agrees."

There was an awkward moment as Christopher kept staring at Faith. Merideth looked on, a bit embarrassed.

Christopher cleared his throat. "Anyway, thank you both for coming in on a Saturday to help. I've been putting off facing the fact that we have to share space with the opera group, but I realized I'd better start thinking about it."

"You'd better do more than think about it, Chris," Merideth came back. "You'd better start taking all the limitations into consideration. Half the things you're doing in rehearsal won't work when you have that *Hansel and Gretel* junk behind you." As if Merideth feared he'd gone too far, he stuffed his hands in his pockets and joked, "Aw, why do today what you can put off until tomorrow. Right?"

Christopher no longer smiled. He rolled down his sleeves and sighed. "I hear you. I wish I had more time to really think about it."

"What the hey," Merideth tossed back. He picked up his scarf and jacket and headed for the exit. "It'll come together. It always does. Somehow."

"Thanks again," Christopher called.

"No problem." Merideth swung his scarf around his neck with great style. "My date for tonight canceled out on me, so it was better to be here than moping around my apartment. I guess I'll see if I can catch a movie. Ciao. See you Monday."

The exit door opened and swung shut. Faith and Christopher were alone.

"Um, I guess I'll go, too," Faith stammered. "My roommate wanted to interview some girls in the dorms. I said I'd help her."

Christopher ignored her half-hearted attempt to leave. "I just don't know how to handle it." His voice had an unsure edge to it, like he really needed someone to talk to.

Faith didn't budge. "What do you mean?"

Chris sat on a rickety stool left behind by the dancers. "They give me a musical to direct, but I have to do it with somebody else's lights and set. For all I know, my actors are going to have to wear witch noses and bread crumbs."

"It'll be okay."

"And the TV station can send someone to come watch rehearsal anytime they like. I'll end up looking like a fool."

"No, you won't. You couldn't."

Christopher turned to gaze up at her and Faith felt as if the molecules in her body were rearranging. The dim light cut his sculptured face in half. He stood up and took a slow step toward her. For that moment everything stopped. The air, the dust, Faith's heart. Then Christopher seemed to stop, too, as if he were putting the brakes on something inside himself. He turned away and walked back to the wings, where he picked up his sport coat and slung it over his arm.

"I should go," he said, not looking at her. "I have to be back at ODT."

"Is there a frat party or something tonight?" Faith asked, hoping to extend the conversation. A moment ago she'd wanted to race away. Now she wanted this stop-time to go on forever.

"Not tonight. Too many people go away for the weekend." For the first time since Faith had met Christopher, his body language wasn't fluid or elegant. He still stood next to the wings, looking over the prop tables and the stage manager's control panel. "I'm, uh, going out to dinner with . . . a friend."

"That sounds nice."

"Mmm. How about you? Have a big weekend

planned with your boyfriend? Didn't you say when we first met that you had a boyfriend?''

Faith couldn't believe that he remembered. She had this weird sense that he was asking more than just a casual question, that Christopher was fishing, trying to find out if she was available. She told herself not to hope. After having been out of circulation for so long, she wasn't very good at picking up cues. This was Christopher Hammond! Not some trombone major who lived in her dorm. "I don't have a boyfriend," she finally said. "Not anymore."

He walked out of the wings, back into the patchy light, closer and closer.

Faith stood staring at him as if he were a ghost. An electrifying buzz was shooting from her forehead to her toes and back again. Then she felt something wind around her waist. No longer aware of the dusty air and the smell of sawdust, she was overwhelmed by starched, crisp cotton and scented, warm skin.

Christopher had one hand on her waist and his other hand was raised, about to touch her hair, or maybe her face. Standing on the middle of the stage like that, Faith felt as if she were in a movie close-up, except that there was no swell of music, no blurry fade-out. It became so quiet that she could hear her own breathing. Every inch of Christopher's face was crystal clear.

He stood close to Faith, looking down at her, smiling. His face came closer and closer to hers. Then he brought down his free hand and produced a tiny pink rose. He tucked the stem into the buttonhole on the strap of her overalls.

Faith tried to catch her breath. She knew that the rose was a prop made of fabric, but it looked amazingly real. That rose held more magic than the most beautiful wildflower in the world.

"I stole it from the prop table," he whispered, laughing just a little. "Don't tell anyone."

"I won't." She put her hand over the rose, feeling the frayed edge. She wondered how many plays the rose had appeared in, and if that tiny flower had ever held as much power as it did right then.

"I'd better go," he said, still standing close. "People . . . are waiting for me. I'll see you Monday."

"Yes."

"Remind me about *Hansel and Gretel*. Merideth was right. I have to start taking it into consideration."

"I will."

He held her by both shoulders for a moment longer, and then he was gone.

"See you Monday," Faith echoed.

She wasn't sure what was happening between her and Christopher, but whatever it was, she was ready for it.

Nine

....

Winnie was nervous. She felt like a grade-schooler going for a ballet audition, or one who'd been called into the principal's office.

She sat outside the counselor's office fiddling with her book bag, which was made of net and had tiny Barbie dolls and pieces of plastic fruit sewn on it. This might be painless, she decided. Just an administrative thing. Drop two classes, check this box, and you're out of here.

But the sinking feeling in Winnie's gut told her otherwise. In high school, she used to get called in for "discussions" about why she wasn't living up to her potential. Once they had called her mother in, too. *That* was great. Her mom looked so professional and about a thousand times more together than Ms. Blumerfeld, the vice principal. After listening to Ms. Blumerfeld's whole spiel, her mom said, "I don't believe in pushing my daughter. Winnie has to take charge of her life when she's ready. You and I need to let her be." After that her mom had sat back with her permissive therapist's smile while Ms. Blumerfeld turned as gray as a piece of sheet metal.

"Winifred Gottlieb?" called a creaky-sounding voice from inside the counselor's office.

Winnie stood up. The plastic figures on her book bag knocked against the little tin ducks on her belt. As she entered the office she took in the dingy room, with its venetian blinds, beige brick walls, and wilting plants. Winnie sat down.

Mr. Morain was a bespectacled, paunchy man wearing a cardigan sweater and sporting a few wispy hairs carefully combed onto the top of his head. "Hello, Winifred."

"You can call me Winnie. Or Winifred. Or whatever you want."

"All right. Winnie." Mr. Morain reached across the desk and produced a manila folder. "I've gone over your transcript, your SAT scores, and your high-school grades."

"Oh, boy," Winnie said.

Mr. Morain peered over his glasses. "You know

your SAT scores are quite high. And so are your achievement scores.'' He creaked forward in his swivel chair, suddenly looking very intense. ''Much better than your grades.''

''Yup.'' Winnie tried to look smug, but she was fumbling. Her stomach was starting to feel like she'd swallowed a block of wood.

''And here it is the first week of school and you've already dropped two courses. Have you decided what to sign up for instead?''

''Not yet.'' Winnie gave a little self-conscious laugh, as if it were all a big joke.

Mr. Morain didn't say anything for a minute. Instead he leaned back in his chair and gave her a thoughtful look. ''Winnie, have you thought about your goals for college? Why are you here? What do you want to get out of this experience?''

Winnie waited, hoping he'd answer his own questions.

He out-waited her.

''I don't know,'' she finally mumbled.

He just sat there with that teacher stare that said, *Keep talking, open your mouth, and step right into my trap.*

Winnie began to ramble. ''Well, you see, actually, my mom and I have this theory. You can't rush into things, especially if you don't know what you're rushing into. Not that I don't rush into some things. I do—but that's a whole other subject. Anyway, as far as school is concerned, I want to give myself time, try different things, and see what happens. There's no point in taking charge of my life if I don't know what I'm taking charge of."

"That's an interesting philosophy," Mr. Morain interrupted. "Unfortunately, I disagree. The way I see it, if you sit and wait for life to happen to you, you may wait for a long, long time. Too long."

"Oh. I see."

Mr. Morain handed Winnie a copy of the fall class schedule. "All right, Winnie. Let's look at your courses. You've decided to stick with French and Western Civ." He glanced up briefly to confirm his deduction. "How about another hard academic class and something a little lighter?" He didn't wait for an answer. "For the lighter side I've got openings in Art Appreciation, Personal Health, or Introduction to Film. Which will it be?"

Winnie sensed that "let me think about it" would be hopeless with this guy. "Uh . . . Introduction to Film."

"Good." He started filling out a computer registration card while still looking over the schedule. "The lit classes I'd like to put you in are all full. How about something in the sciences?"

Winnie slunk lower.

"Maybe next term." He smiled. "How about something else in the history department? I know you're already in Western Civ, but that might make it more interesting. Let's see what's open. You do like history?''

"Sure." Winnie did think that history was less boring than a lot of subjects. Like accounting. Or logic.

"Okay. History of Russia. It's an honors class, but that'll be good for you."

"Honors! I'm not in Honors College."

Mr. Morain leaned back in his chair and scratched the top of his balding head. "Don't worry about that," he said. "I can make exceptions for students who have special circumstances."

Winnie wanted to crawl under the chair. Honors College classes were for the brightest, most motivated students. Brooks was in the Honors College. Melissa took honors biology, and she said she had twice the homework of a freshman in regular Biology 100.

"So it's settled." He slid over two registration cards for Winnie to sign.

For once in her life, Winnie didn't say a word. She felt like she'd just been shanghaied.

Varoom, varoom.
Steven Garth's Batmobile tipped on corners. It was noisier than a pneumatic drill. It had been jury-rigged so that the dash looked like a telephone switchboard. And KC sat so low in the passenger seat, she felt like asking for a phone book.

"What's Bernhard's address, partner?" Steven asked her a few hours later on that same Monday.

KC wasn't sure which name was more obnoxious, "little angel" or "partner." "A Street and Seventeenth," she spat back. "Go straight. It's on the other side of the railroad tracks."

"The other side of the tracks," Steven teased, flicking back his hair and grinning. "I've always been intrigued by the other side of tracks. How about you?"

"Not particularly."

The Corvette rounded another corner, making KC feel like the car was balanced on one wheel. After meeting Steven downtown, they still had a two-mile trek over to Bernhard's. KC would have felt weird chauffeuring Steven in a borrowed BMW, so she'd ended up leaving the car near The Strand. But she felt like a prisoner going for a joyride in Steven's black Corvette.

The corner of A and Seventeenth streets was in view. It was in the old section of Springfield, block after block of ancient warehouses bordering the river. Steven sped down and parked in front of an old, low building that had a tiny sign identifying it as Bernhard's Wholesale Athletic Supplies.

"Here we are, partner." He winked at her in the rear view mirror.

KC glared back at his reflection. At least she knew she looked great. The green jacket set off her gray eyes and looked perfect with her black pleated skirt and patent-leather shoes. In contrast, Steven was wearing crinkled khakis and a heavy fisherman's sweater. Although KC couldn't see more than the collar of the shirt he had on underneath, she knew it hadn't been ironed. He hadn't bothered to get a haircut, and his bare ankles flashed between his loafers and his rumpled pants.

"I hope you brought our business checkbook?" he asked as they got out of the car and trotted up the metal steps.

"Of course."

"What's our name again?"

"Soccer, Inc."

"Right. Very original. Soccer, Inc."

"What was I supposed to call it? Ice Capades and Friends?" KC stopped on the steps and faced him. "Look, Garth Petroleum. I know you think you're God's gift to business, but once we go inside this building, would you please not make fun of me or tell me I'm doing something stupid? Because in case you haven't heard, part of business is making a good impression. And as you said yourself, we *are* partners—gag—so we'd better act like partners!"

Steven didn't grin. For a moment he didn't say anything. He thought, rubbed his chin, and thought some more.

Finally he said, "You know, KC, I'm not the only

one who's always egging things on. If you'll recall, you yelled at me first that night we almost wrecked each others' cars. It's always been your game. I'm just more than willing to play—I figure it's either that or nothing at all. You know, you're about as easy to get to know as a refrigerated truck. Give a guy a break.''

All the mockery was gone from Steven's face. He was looking at her with direct dark eyes, which were somehow even more challenging than when he grinned and taunted her.

She felt confused and off balance as she turned away. She pushed on the glass warehouse door, which jangled a little bell tied to the door handle. KC strode in. The warehouse was so plain it looked unfinished. The walls were white and fluorescent light fixtures ran along the ceilings. The only decoration was a framed picture of the original Mr. Bernhard. He wore a mustache and a striped rugby shirt—probably the first shirt his factory had ever made.

A receptionist was at a table piled with inventory sheets and order forms.

''Yeah?'' the receptionist barked when KC and Steven approached. She was talking into the phone and barely paused from her conversation.

Steven gestured for KC to take charge. Actually, he backed up and made a little bow.

''We have an appointment to see Mr. Kusher about

soccer shirts," KC explained, trying not to let her irritation with Steven color her voice.

"Down the hall," the receptionist grunted, pointing with her pencil.

KC and Steven went down the hall and then into a football-field-sized room with dirty windows. They heard the repetitive whirr of sewing machines. There were big tables where patterns were being cut, racks of baseball jackets, and a wall covered with insignia designs. Scraps of fabric littered the floor, along with discarded buttons, decorative letters, bits of elastic, and plastic bags.

The place was busy and crowded. Everyone was either sewing, cutting, pushing racks, checking lists, or marking off forms on clipboards. Many wore Walkmans, and those who didn't laughed and chattered loudly. KC took an unconscious step back toward Steven. In such a strange, almost hostile environment, she actually felt like he was an ally.

Steven moved forward until his shoulder was against KC's back. For a moment they stood there, too aware of each other and not doing a thing.

Finally Steven lunged away and tapped a Walkmanned worker. "We're here to see Mr. Kusher. Can you point him out?"

The cutter pointed out a skinny young man checking wrestling suits on the rack nearest the opposite wall.

Steven led the way over, but KC walked fast, over-taking him.

"Mr. Kusher," KC said in a loud voice, thrusting out her hand, "I'm KC Angeletti. I talked to you on the phone about getting soccer shirts made for the U of S dorm teams."

Mr. Kusher ignored her attempt to shake hands. He shrugged, as if to say, *Big deal. So?*

"We'd like to pick up some samples to show people, and then we can come back with an order," Steven affirmed.

Mr. Kusher stopped his work for the merest second, grabbed a notebook with plastic-laminated pages, opened it to the section marked *soccer*, and handed it to KC.

"Let me know which ones you want. Prices are on the bottom," Mr. Kusher said. He went back to his work.

KC set the notebook on an unused cutting table. There were six different styles of soccer jersey, and each was available in a dozen colors. "I guess we can afford to get four samples," KC said, noting the price.

"We should get more than that," Steven insisted. He was standing very close to her again, examining the page with great concentration. "We should get one of each style. All six."

"We only have enough money in our account for

four," KC reminded him. "Four samples will be enough."

Steven started to take out his wallet, then remembered. "Hey, partner, why should I make up the difference? You're the one who owes the kitty. Why don't you pitch in here?"

"Okay," KC came back, not knowing how she was going to get out of it again. She wondered if she shouldn't have asked to borrow some money from Lauren, rather than just her car. She started for her empty wallet, then pretended to explode with anger. "It just bugs me that he's so uninterested in us. It's like he's doing us some big favor by letting us buy his shirts!"

"KC, he thinks we're rinky-dink. He thinks we want to take up his whole afternoon to order four shirts."

"Well, he's wrong," KC said, managing to turn her panic to indignation. She couldn't quite look Steven in the face, so she turned away and went back to Mr. Kusher.

"Excuse me, Mr. Kusher," she said loudly.

Mr. Kusher put down his clipboard and stared at her.

KC thought fast. She remembered nearly missing her chance to bargain over her green jacket, and wondered if that might not be the way to go. "You know, this is the first year that the intramural dorm league is ordering uniforms, but if this catches on it will certainly become a tradition. And the dorm leagues don't just play soccer. There's intramural softball. Uh, basketball, too," she improvised. "And we'd like all those uniforms to come from Bernhard's." She felt Steven come right up behind her shoulder again. His floppy hair lightly brushed her cheek. "That is, if we can work out the right deal."

Mr. Kusher suddenly looked more interested. "What do you need?"

"We think you could at least throw in an extra sample shirt . . . or two. After all, we'll be showing these shirts to hundreds of students. Hundreds. And we want to make sure we have enough to go around."

Mr. Kusher thought for a moment. The vision of hundreds of soccer shirts flying out of his factory was obviously changing his attitude. "All right, I'll throw in two more sample shirts, no charge. And if you come back with over twenty-five orders I'll give you a ten-percent discount."

"And if we come back with over fifty orders, you'll give us a twenty-percent break. Right?" dared Steven.

"Fifteen," Mr. Kusher came back.

"Twenty," KC and Steven said at the same time.

"Or else we take our business elsewhere," KC added.

Mr. Kusher smiled. "Twenty." Then he went to

his back room, returning with six shirts in plastic bags. He handed them to Steven while KC wrote him a Soccer, Inc. check. Mr. Kusher marked his discount deal down on the receipt and gave it to KC.

"Thank you," KC said.

"Thanks for your business," he replied.

With great dignity and control, KC and Steven walked back out of the workroom, past the receptionist, and down the metal steps. But as soon as they were safely out in the street, they ran and leaped with glee.

"All right, little angel!" Steven shouted. He had shirts tucked under one arm, but held his other palm in the air.

KC was exploding with triumph. For once she forgot about being broke, about missing out on a sorority. She even forgot that she didn't like Steven Garth. She slapped Steven's palm as hard as she could and screamed, "*Yes!* Are we brilliant?"

"Yes!"

"Are we geniuses?"

"Yes!"

"Are we the best?"

"The best, partner. *The best!*"

Before KC really knew it, she was in Steven's arms, jumping up and down like a little kid while he clutched her waist, his arms winding round her and holding on hard.

As soon as KC was aware that her arms were up around his neck, she gasped and pulled away. They stared at each other, and for that single second neither of them could come up with a taunt, a jab, or a joke.

"So, what now?" Steven asked, his voice suddenly soft.

"What do you mean?" KC responded, feeling wobbly and strange.

He turned away, almost as if he were embarrassed, and unlocked the door to his car. "Shall we go celebrate?"

"Right now?"

"Now or never."

"I have a class."

Steven slid into the driver's seat, then opened the door for her. "You do?" he asked after she'd sat down.

KC felt too close all of a sudden. The car seemed too small, too intimate.

He leaned over and touched her arm. "Are you just trying to drive me crazy, Angeletti, or do you really have a class?"

"Accounting. Three o'clock."

"I guess we'd better go back."

"I guess so."

Steven started the Corvette. He took one last look

at her, then sighed and pounded the steering wheel. "Okay. I guess I'll see you in class tomorrow."

"Yes."

"We'll show the samples to Helen and Edward."

"Yes."

"And figure out where to go from there."

"We will."

They drove back to The Strand in a funny silence, smiling at each other every once in a while but not saying anything.

KC quickly walked back to Lauren's car. She had a vision of herself turning around and running back to Steven. But she didn't do it. Instead she fumbled with Lauren's keys. She couldn't get the door unlocked and she almost dropped her briefcase. But it didn't bother her in the least.

As KC drove back to the dorm, she realized that she was still thinking about Steven, and she was in a very good mood.

Ten

The second week of classes was coming to an end. Football season began. Leaves piled up. Freshmen were getting in the groove. People were on time for breakfast. Winnie remembered her meal pass. Faith, Winnie, and KC met for their afternoon soap opera every day, and Winnie's dorm had gone two straight nights without a party.

But for Lauren, college wasn't getting any easier. That week Marielle had dragged her to an aerobics class, where she'd almost vomited doing high kicks. She'd conducted two interviews with dorm dwellers, which hadn't been much more productive than talking to the sorority pledges. The only good thing that had happened was reading her childhood piece aloud in writing lab and having the prof say it was "in the right direction."

"Lauren, what are you doing?" Faith asked.

It was Thursday evening and all four girls were together again in Faith and Lauren's room. That was something else that had become routine—using that room as their meeting place. The three old friends hung out there, while Lauren sat like an uninvited guest, never sure if she was the fourth to make up a perfect square, or the one outside the triangle who would never, ever fit.

That evening, Faith sat cross-legged in the corner, reading some avant-garde play she'd borrowed from an actor downstairs. She was beginning to look more collegy all of a sudden. Maybe it was the addition of a hand-print vest she'd borrowed from their neighbor. She'd just unbraided her hair, and while it flowed over her shoulders, it still held its evenly spaced kinks.

"I'm not doing anything important," Lauren said. No matter what kind of transformation Marielle was hoping to put her through, she was still the same old Lauren. She sat at her desk in a tweed skirt and beige cashmere sweater, feeling blobby and overdressed.

KC lay on Faith's bed, her Soccer, Inc. orders spread out in front of her. She had on one of her sample soccer shirts over her good black dress. "It looks like you're addressing invitations to a birthday party."

"They're just thank-you notes to the people I interviewed for my article. I delivered most of them this morning. These are the last few."

Winnie was at Faith's desk, staring into a textbook as if her life depended on it. "Well, don't bother sending them to the beasts in my dorm," she said, barely looking up. "The pizzas you treated them to were more than enough."

Faith suddenly put down her script and looked at KC. "How are sales?" There was a funny, uncharacteristic edge to her voice.

"We've sold thirty-seven shirts so far." KC held up a brown paper sack full of bills. "That's three hundred and seventy dollars. We have to make it to fifty shirts at least, though."

"Did Brooks order one?" Faith asked, frustration finally showing through her placid smile.

"Gee, I don't know. I think he did."

"How's he doing?"

KC pretended to look through her records as if she had no idea what Faith was talking about.

"He's head of the soccer league," Faith insisted, putting her play script aside. "I'm sure you've talked to him about this shirt thing. Maybe you talked to him about some other things, too. I just wish you would tell me."

"Look, if you two don't want to talk to each

other," KC pointed out, "that's up to you. Don't drag me into it. Brooks is still my friend."

"I know." Faith huffed. "I'm sorry."

Lauren tried to ease the sudden tension and make contact with KC. "I bet you'll sell a lot more than fifty, KC," she offered. "If some people on the teams have nice jerseys, everyone else will want them, too."

KC was finally looking at Lauren with some warmth and a little relief when they were all distracted by a knock at the door.

"Who's that?" Lauren had the sickening feeling that it was Marielle, dropping off a diet plan or a book on choosing your colors.

"The masked intruder," Winnie quipped. "He's come to rescue me from Russian history. *Save me*," she hollered.

Faith called, "Who is it?" but she couldn't make out the reply.

Winnie looked back at Lauren. "Maybe somebody decided to pay you back, treating you to a pizza and having it delivered. Faith, do you remember when KC and I did that to you in high school? When we sent that pizza to you and Brooks after the—" Winnie clapped her hand over her mouth. "Oops."

That made Lauren wonder if it were Brooks at the door.

"Come in," Faith invited. "It's open."

It wasn't Marielle. And it wasn't Brooks.

It was Christopher Hammond.

He didn't wait to be asked in. His six-foot frame strode in. There was a frantic look in his eyes, as if he were there to deliver bad news. And yet he was dressed like he'd just come from a formal party. He'd left his jacket behind, but wore charcoal suit slacks, a tie, and a starched pink shirt with cuff links. Instantly he recognized Lauren, and both of them stared at the floor.

"Sorry to bother you." He transferred his elegant, somewhat panicked gaze to Faith.

Lauren felt even sicker than if it had been Marielle. Seeing Christopher again made it all come flooding back: How she'd been fixed up with Christopher for the Dream Date Dance, how it had turned out to be the Trash Your Roommate Dance instead, how Christopher's roommate, Mark, had fixed him up with the girl he thought was the most unsightly and worthless—the girl whose feelings were worth throwing away. Lauren Turnbell-Smythe.

Christopher blurted, "I need to talk to Faith."

Lauren saw Faith rise from her corner as if she were being lifted by strings.

Christopher met Faith in the middle of the room. He hesitated for a moment, as if he would have preferred privacy, then explained, "I'm in trouble."

"What happened?" Faith had to know.

KC and Winnie stared, blatantly eavesdropping.

Christopher explained in a rush. "The station manager from KYSU is coming to watch rehearsal tomorrow. I was sure she wouldn't come to watch for weeks! Weeks! I only found out she's coming tomorrow because her son is pledging my fraternity and he let me know to show his loyalty to my house." He paused to catch his breath and Faith reassuringly touched his arm.

KC stared harder.

"She's going to see me rehearsing against all that *Hansel and Gretel* junk. Nothing we've rehearsed so far will make any sense. And then she's going to ask me how I plan to adjust to that awful set, and I'm going to tell her that I really don't know. I haven't seriously thought about it yet. And she's going to laugh in my face and know that anybody she'd want as an apprentice would have had this all figured out before the first rehearsal. I'm going to look like a jerk."

Faith turned away from him, and for a moment he looked even more distraught. But then she was with him again, a few theater magazines in hand, along with a sketch pad and her fringed suede jacket. "Do you have your directing script?"

"It's back at the house."

"Can we get into the theater?"

"No. Not tonight."

Faith suddenly looked possessed, as if she could

lead an army. "Can you get in touch with Joe and Gretchen? We won't need the dancers. Almost everything depends on the two leads."

"I can probably find them. Gretchen lives in this dorm."

"We'll find them." Faith was leading him to the door. "We'll all go to your frat house. There must be a big room there we can use. We'll go over everything, from beginning to end, and make it work."

"How?"

"We'll figure it out," Faith said, leading him out. There was a determined smile on her face, plus an airy lift to her posture and a dazed, I'll-follow-you-anywhere look in her eye. "It may take all night, but we'll figure it out."

Before Faith could reach the door, KC was on her feet. "Faith, I need to tell you something." Her tone was secretive and very strange.

Faith looked back at KC as if her friend had lost her mind. "I'll find you tomorrow."

"Let's go, Faith," Christopher urged. "I'll call Joe if you'll go down the hall and find Gretchen."

KC tried once more to get Faith's attention, but it was too late. Faith and Christopher were gone.

The room was quiet, as if a cyclone had just blown through. KC seemed to be assessing serious damage. But Lauren wasn't sure what that damage was.

Furiously, KC collected her Soccer, Inc. orders and

stuffed them in her briefcase. "Come on, Win," she ordered. "Let's go back to our dorms."

Winnie was still squinting at her history book, but KC already had her blazer on and was heading for the door. Lauren had the feeling that something important had just happened, something too important to discuss with her. She felt as if she'd done something terribly wrong, even though she sensed that KC's sudden exit had nothing to do with her. It had to do with Faith. And Christopher.

"What's the matter?" Lauren managed to ask as Winnie finally joined KC at the door.

KC frowned.

"Bye, Lauren," said Winnie.

"It's nothing, Lauren," KC finally answered. She stared down the hall.

"Nothing," Lauren repeated after she'd been left alone. "Or none of my business."

"Honors history. Yuck."

Winnie was back in her dorm room, also alone. She wasn't quite sure, either, why KC had suddenly acted so flipped-out. On the way home KC had said something about not wanting Faith to get hurt. But Winnie hadn't followed it because her mind was too full of Russian history and early American film.

By the time Winnie had taken off her jumper and all her scarves she'd completely stopped worrying about KC, because she had to study. She had four history chapters to catch up on. And although her Russian history lectures had been interesting, her textbook was as dry and boring as unbuttered toast.

Hoping to make something sink in, Winnie stretched out on the floor and read out loud. Melissa was out, at a seminar on "Using Your Mental Powers." The seminar was supposed to help Melissa's track performance, but from what Winnie had seen, Melissa used her mental powers just fine. She could probably clean up their dorm room just by thinking "neat."

Winnie was glad to have the room to herself, but soon she was daydreaming. Kicking her feet in the air, painting imaginary shapes with her green felt shoes, thinking about Josh, her mother, and her trip that past summer to France. Before she knew it, she had flipped through a whole chapter in her textbook and gone from the fall of Kiev to the rise of Moscow without having absorbed a thing.

Winnie rolled over and put her book on top of her head. Deep down, she wanted to find something that interested her. She wanted to "reach her potential." She just wasn't sure what it had to do with Moscow and the Mongols and the fall of the Kievan state.

"If you don't know what to do about it, then do something else for a while," she joked out loud, getting up again and examining one of the anatomy models on Melissa's side of the room.

Then she ordered herself, as if she were a military recruit, "Take a break, Gottlieb. Go down to the basement, get some really gross junk food, come back and study all night. Yes, sir! I mean, yes, ma'am!" She checked her shoe for quarters and went out.

It was Winnie's lucky night. She made it downstairs without getting mauled, harassed, whistled at, invited in, blasted, distracted, or pelted by water balloons. Someone had taped a sheet of notebook paper with the word *poison* scrawled on it to the basement candy machine. And someone else had added beneath that *lighten up*.

Winnie slipped coins in and watched the snacks tumble down. A Snickers bar. Peanuts. Lifesavers. Something called a Marsh Mellow that looked really gooey and sweet. She was leaning over to collect her loot when she heard footsteps.

"Hey." It was Josh.

"Hi," she stammered. She clutched her armload of nuts and candy, wishing that she could do a swift turn and dump it all in a washing machine. She was wearing just her purple tights, felt shoes, and a huge T-shirt that came to the middle of her thighs. She felt like she'd just walked into the men's bathroom stark naked with a dried mud mask on her face.

"I missed dinner," she lied, trying to hide the candy.

"How've you been?" Josh responded. He didn't look totally together, either. His dark hair needed combing; a button was missing from his denim shirt; his sweater was moth-eaten around the collar; his heels were flapping over the backs of his moccasins; and he wasn't even wearing his earring.

"I've been okay," Winnie answered. Something was clunking around in a nearby dryer, maybe a tennis shoe or a throw rug. The rhythmic *thunk* made Winnie feel like there was a microphone attached to her heart.

Josh's deep-set eyes looked sleepy, which Winnie thought was unusual. Although, if she really thought about it, she had to admit that she didn't know Josh well enough to say what was usual and what was not. A sharp ping of pain went off inside her.

"Studying?" Josh asked. He bought an Almond Joy for himself, then put coins in the next machine to get a Coke.

"I'm trying."

"Me, too." There was another *thunk-clunk* as the Coke can dropped. Josh fished the soda out. "Computer majors are all sugar junkies. We stay up all night barely surviving on moon pies and Twinkies."

Winnie finally showed him her stash. "Undeclared majors do the same thing." She was getting a tiny, hopeful sense that he might be as embarrassed, as caught off guard as she. For some reason, she didn't feel quite as awful as she'd thought she would.

"Or maybe it's just being a freshman."

"What's that?"

"Staying up all night." He opened the can and took a swig of Coke. "Living on sugar and caffeine. Feeling like everything is just a little beyond you, and you're not quite sure how to catch up."

Winnie knew he was trying to talk about something more personal than proper nutrition. "Maybe it's freshmanitis."

"What?"

"Remember senioritis in high school? That irresistible urge to cut class and go to the beach, or shred up all the school's typing paper and throw it in the air like confetti? Come to think of it, I think I had junioritis, sophomoritis . . ."

"Preschoolitis."

"Really."

They laughed.

He sat down on the bench near the soda machine. For a moment he seemed to be collecting his thoughts. He played with his woven bracelet and stared at it. He looked even thinner than the last time Winnie had seen him, as if he were already burning the candle at both ends. "Anyway, it's good to see you again. I, uh, felt kind of weird after orientation week."

"Don't worry about it," Winnie bluffed. "Nothing happened. I passed out in your room, that's all."

"I just wasn't quite sure what to say to you after that," he explained slowly. "I guess that first week, everybody's in such a hurry to get to know people and, well, things can get weird pretty fast."

Winnie felt something cave in inside, and yet she continued to stand tall. She knew what Josh was saying: *Just because you passed out in my room and assumed we'd slept together doesn't mean anything really happened between us. And I kept my distance afterward to make sure you figured that out.*

Oh, I figured it out, Winnie wanted to tell him. *I've started to figure out quite a few things since I arrived at U of S.*

"I totally understand," she managed. "I feel the same way." She stuck out her hand to shake his. "So let's leave orientation behind us now that we're full-fledged freshmen." She couldn't quite believe she was pulling it off, because her insides were still stinging. "What do you say?"

Josh shook her hand. Then he jumped up and nudged her with his shoulder. "Hey, how'd you like to go to this restaurant just off campus called The Zero Bagel? It's where all the computer eggheads hang out. The food's terrible, but the music's okay. And the best part is, nobody cares how you dress. We can just talk and hang out. It's one of those nights when I really need to get away from the dorm."

Winnie thought for a moment. *Was having Josh as a dorm buddy better than thinking of him as a failed romance and a distraction? Yes. It probably was.*

"Do they require pants?" she joked, referring to her T-shirt and tights.

"Nah. Just tie this around your waist." He gave her his moth-eaten sweater. "We can eat this really bad goulash and play some pool."

"Gee. How can I resist?"

"You can't." They headed for the stairs. "So tell me about your classes," he said as they hiked up.

Winnie marveled at how comfortable they were with each other all of a sudden.

"I transferred into two new courses," she mentioned. "One's in the Honors College."

"Yeah? Great. What is it?"

"Russian History. We're starting with the medieval period. No wait, I think we're even before that."

Josh laughed, then offered Winnie a sip of his Coke as they stepped outside. It was a mild night, clear with no stars. The mountain air was cool and clean. "Medieval Russia. I bet the guys look like they're in ZZ Top."

"Yeah," Winnie admitted. "But you probably wouldn't want to dance with them."

Josh laughed and slipped his arm around her as they walked away from the green. It wasn't a romantic over the shoulder caress, but Winnie didn't care. She slung her arm around his narrow waist in a friendly fashion, too. Why not, she decided. For that night, just friends was A Okay with her.

Dorm life.

It was almost eleven and every version of "Dorm Life" Lauren had written so far looked duller than the draft before. She'd tried everything to get her imagination going: free writing, blank verse, doing the whole article as if it were a cartoon or a top-forty song. She'd even tried eavesdropping on her dorm neighbors to get a line of dialogue, an expression, anything that would create a spark. At least Faith hadn't come back and wasn't there to see her sweat and strain.

Lauren resorted to wandering up and down the second-floor hall. She felt like the dorm phantom. Her body slept in Coleridge Hall, took showers, ate microwave popcorn. Her luggage lived in Coleridge, along with her TV and VCR, her computer, her collection of CDs, and her expensive wheat-colored woolens. But her spirit was somewhere else entirely. Not at the Tri Beta house, that was for sure, but somewhere far away from her heavy limbs, her clumsy good clothes, her stifling mother, and her awkward new home.

Lauren stopped, sensing that she was beginning to get the kernel of an idea. Something to do with being a phantom, with walking alone in a place where everyone was supposed to feel so together. Just then she heard voices coming from the open door of a double room. More than two voices. A late-night mini-get-together. And they all sounded like they were in a crazy mood.

"What is that? Oh, no!" one girl groaned.

Lauren thought she recognized the sound of Freya's voice. She was the opera singer from Germany who lived next door with Kimberly. But she only half paid attention as she silently padded by. The giddy conversation continued.

"Not the dreaded thank-you note!" said another girl. "I got mine yesterday."

"From Lauren Turnbell-Smythe?"

"My note thanked me for being so helpful and expressing myself so well! And I didn't say a word. I just sat there eating her pizza."

"It's sad."

Lauren stopped. As much as she wanted to run away from the talk, she felt a need to know what people really thought of her. Her feet stayed planted near the open room.

"Melody, shh. Lauren's nice."

"I know. But boy, does she throw her money around."

"She's just insecure."

"Yeah. I wouldn't mind being that insecure."

A loud burst of laughter was followed by a sudden silence and then muffled giggles, as if the girls knew that someone had heard them. Lauren practically ran back to her room.

She locked her door, went over to her CD player, and turned it on as loud as it would go. Then she turned on her TV at high volume, knowing full well that it was strictly against the quiet rules and that the RA would be up there in about five minutes. But at least in those five minutes there would be enough noise coming from her room so that no one would hear her scream.

"*Aaahhh!*" Lauren wailed, throwing herself on her bed. It wasn't fair! It wasn't right! How could anyone try as hard as she did and still be an object of scorn?

Maybe that was it, she realized, sitting up again and turning down the noise. She tried too hard. She gave too much. Even Dash Ramirez probably had smelled it on her the minute she walked into his office.

Lauren went back over to her computer and reread the last draft of her article. It sounded as phony and smarmy as the people who'd talked to her. She

pressed the delete key and watched all her work disappear. *Highlight. Zap.* Good riddance and farewell.

*Why does living together make some freshmen feel so
alone?* she suddenly began instead.

Her fingers flying over the keyboard, Lauren began
to write and write and write.

Eleven

·····························

Hey, KC, I've been looking for you. Can I get one of those soccer shirts?"

"You sure can." KC waited for Dan Atkinson, a goalie who lived in Brooks' dorm. He was a fitness fanatic, running in a Gore-Tex jogging suit on the rainy, blustery morning. Changing his course to run over, Dan pulled an order slip and money out of his fanny pack.

"Thanks, Dan."

"It's a good deal. Hey, make sure I get the red lettering."

"Don't worry. I will."

Dan saluted and began running toward the library. KC went in the opposite direction. She was headed to the bank. Dan's order would certainly be her last and she was eager to deposit the cash she'd collected that week—four hundred and sixty dollars. Since it was Friday, KC wanted the Soccer, Inc. money safely stowed for the weekend. She didn't want to put it under her mattress or—even worse—ask help from Steven, who probably had a Swiss bank account or his own personal wall safe.

Steven. KC found herself thinking about Steven as she carefully sidestepped puddles and mud, passing the science center and the ROTC building. She kept telling herself to just buzz him off, like she'd done to every other guy who'd driven her crazy. But this was a different kind of crazy. That kind of crazy made her picture his face about every ten minutes, made her think back to something he'd said or remember the way he'd come up behind her, his shoulder brushing against hers. She kept recalling the way they had worked as a team down at Bernhard's. It had almost been . . . exciting.

"Get out of my brain, Garth," she demanded, hammering her legs down and moving fast. "Excitement is not what I'm interested in." She passed the health center, crossed University Avenue, and walked into the bank. "You are just an accident, a distraction who happens to be in my business class. You don't matter!"

KC didn't realize how hard she was stomping until

she heard her patent-leather flats clicking across the bank's linoleum floor. It was only ten-thirty, so the campus branch wasn't too crowded. The big ficus trees looked freshly watered and the ski photos peered down at her, along with the cameras that were supposed to take pictures of robbers. *They should have a camera to take pictures of successful business customers, too,* KC told herself as she proudly got into the teller line.

Out of the corner of her eye KC saw Pamela Myers, and she offered a confident smile. But Ms. Myers was too busy searching through her desk to smile back. If the bank officer hadn't been so busy, KC would have gone over and boasted about the success of Soccer, Inc. She wanted everyone in the world to know that Kahia Cayanne Angeletti was not destined to be just like her parents, scraping by with a crummy health-food restaurant, owing money to everyone and pretending that they'd always planned to live that way. No, KC Angeletti was going to be as successful as she looked that morning in her new green jacket, waiting to make a large deposit at the campus bank.

Someone got in line behind KC. She was writing a check so she didn't notice those around her. But KC noticed her and wasn't sure how to react. She wished she could magically disappear, but there was nowhere to go, nowhere to hide. She was going to have to talk to Courtney Conner, the head of the Tri Beta sorority.

Courtney was actually wearing jeans. Of course, they were elegant designer jeans matched with a refined checker blouse. It must have been laundry day at the Tri Beta sorority, or the one morning all year when sisters dressed down to repaint the bathrooms.

Courtney finished filling out her check and lifted her blond head. When she saw KC, her eyes registered surprise and a touch of embarrassment, soon replaced by warm politeness.

"Hello, KC." As usual her voice was gracious and honey-smooth. "How nice to see you."

"Hello." KC managed to smile. If she had to run into Courtney again, this was as good a time as any. Maybe she could drop a few hints about the success of Soccer, Inc.

"How are your classes?" Courtney asked.

"Great. The best." There was no way that KC wanted to present herself as anything but deliriously happy. She would rather have quit school than admit she still had nightmares about not becoming a Tri Beta. "How are your classes?"

"Terrific."

"That's good."

"I have a wonderful schedule this semester."

The line chugged ahead. "How's everyone at the sorority house?"

"Busy. Very busy."

It was like having a conversation in a foreign language. No matter what came out of her mouth, all KC could do was wonder how she was coming off and what Courtney thought of her.

"We're starting to plan for Greek Week and homecoming, of course." Courtney let out a little sigh. She bit her lip. "You know, KC, it's too bad rush turned out the way it did. I still think you would have made a terrific Tri Beta. You know I was pushing for you. But sometimes things just don't work out the way you plan."

"It's okay. Now that classes have started, I've realized that I'm too busy to have time for something like a sorority," KC bluffed. "So it's just as well."

"I'm glad you feel that way. No hard feelings?"

"Oh, no."

"Good."

KC had to admit that Courtney had always behaved decently toward her. Unlike Marielle, Courtney had even been friendly to Lauren. And she never would have dropped KC if KC hadn't forced the issue by insulting Mark Geisslinger and Marielle.

KC and Courtney both craned to see why the teller line had stopped moving. A couple of business customers were at the counter, counting out big stacks of checks and bills. KC hoped that Courtney would be able to see her pull out that kind of deposit as well.

But then, as they waited and smiled and listened

to the faint tinkle of Muzak, KC remembered something else that was almost as important to her as Soccer, Inc. and impressing Courtney.

"Courtney, you know Christopher Hammond, don't you?"

"Of course. Why?"

KC had to phrase this with care. The last thing she wanted was to insinuate that *she* was infatuated with Christopher. "Well, last Friday I saw him with his girlfriend—at least I assume it was his girlfriend." KC paused, giving Courtney a chance to say, *No, he doesn't have a girlfriend.* "She looked so familiar. I think I know her from somewhere. Maybe high-school debating or leadership camp—it's been driving me crazy. Do you know her name?"

The line finally started to move ahead again.

"Her name . . ." Courtney struggled to recall. "I can't remember. She goes to Mills College in California, but she still comes out here every other weekend. They're engaged. What *is* her name?"

Christopher was engaged! And from what KC had seen the previous night, Faith was completely gone over him. Christopher was going to tear Faith's inexperienced heart into shreds!

But KC certainly wasn't going to explain that to Courtney. Actually, it was her turn to approach the teller. But before she made it to the counter, she was intercepted by Pamela Myers.

"Kahia, I have to talk to you," Ms. Myers said. "Could you please come over to my desk?"

"I guess so."

"I'll take care of any teller business for you."

With Courtney watching her every move, KC followed the bank officer. They both sat down. For a few moments, Ms. Myers shuffled through the papers on her desk, finally coming up with a computer print-out with KC's name on the top.

"It says here that you've already gone way over your limit on your Western Charge Card," Ms. Myers stated bluntly. "I'm afraid we'll have to cancel your card and set up a payment schedule." She tried to smile. "When it's all paid off, Kahia, we can talk about reopening it and trying again. It's not unusual for students to go overboard the first time they have credit. But we take it seriously."

A two-fold wave of terror went through KC. First, because of being caught by Ms. Myers, and doubly awful, because she sensed that someone was standing behind her chair, someone who had just overheard the whole humiliating interlude.

Ms. Myers was staring up behind KC, acknowledging that yes, someone was indeed standing there.

The bank officer pushed back her chair. "I need to get a payment schedule sheet. I'll be right back."

KC turned.

Courtney was standing right behind her.

KC wanted to crawl into the pocket of her new green jacket.

"I didn't mean to eavesdrop," Courtney insisted, a little red-faced. "I just remembered what Christopher's fiancée's name is. Suzanna Pennerman." When KC couldn't hide her distress, Courtney added in a soft, chummy voice, "I did the same thing with my first credit card. But you know what? If you just pay the whole thing off right away, not only do they forgive you, they raise your limit!"

KC was mortified. At that moment she would have done anything to convince Courtney she wasn't a loser. She opened her briefcase and fingered the Soccer, Inc. money.

"I know," KC responded, trying to sound just as chummy and smug. "That's why I did it. They'd only give me two hundred dollars of credit. So I thought I'd make them push it up. I mean, what can you get for two hundred dollars?"

"Really." Courtney laughed. She gave KC a conspiratorial little hug, then tiptoed away when Ms. Myers finally returned.

Ms. Myers showed KC the payment schedule.

But before she could explain it, KC said, "That won't be necessary."

"Oh?"

"I'd like to pay the whole thing off. That was my intention all along."

KC counted out three hundred and eighty dollars from her Soccer, Inc. fund, ignored the sickening feeling in her stomach, and handed it over to pay off her Western Charge.

Faith blinked her eyes. She yawned. She shivered and laughed, unable to walk a straight line. Her head and her limbs were like rubber. She wondered if this was how it felt to be drunk. She wondered if this was how it felt to be madly in love. She'd never felt this way with Brooks, and she'd thought she'd been in love with him. All she knew was that she hadn't slept all night and if she didn't get some rest soon, she was going to get totally loony.

"Are you as wasted as I am?" Christopher asked, laughing and swaying, too. They were walking through the morning rain, and he was letting it pour down his face. His once-crisp shirt was glued to his chest. "I think the last time I stayed awake for an entire night was when I pledged ODT, three years ago."

Faith giggled. She'd never stayed up all night before. Even on prom night with Brooks, she'd been home and asleep by four A.M. But this was a day of firsts, a year of firsts, the start of a lifetime of trying things that were new.

Christopher was walking her back to her dorm and they were stumbling across the green. Everyone else looked so mundane with their umbrellas and note-books, as if this were an ordinary Friday morning. Yet Faith felt as if she were walking upside down. Swimming to the moon. She headed right for a wooden bench, not aware of what she was doing until Christopher looped his arm through hers at the last minute and detoured her around it.

"Thanks." She wiped away rain. Her hair flowed down her back and shoulders like seaweed. "I needed that."

"I know." He kept a firm hold on her arm. "You're the one who deserves thanks."

They started walking in step, as if they were a dance team.

"All I did was pay attention during rehearsal," Faith said. "Every time you set blocking or staged a song, I'd just think, how does this have to be changed to work on that dumb *Hansel and Gretel* set?"

"Why didn't I think that way?"

Faith grinned. "Because you're not an overly-eager-to-please freshman."

"Is that what you are?"

She nudged him, almost knocking him over. She was amazed how exhaustion had loosened her inhibitions. Of course, after staying up all night with Christopher, it was hard to still think of him as an untouchable Bee Moc. Not after they'd spent over fourteen straight hours together, brainstorming, shoving furniture, humming songs off key, going over every scene in *Stop the World* until Faith knew the lines as well as the actors.

"Do you think Joe and Gretchen will remember everything?" Christopher worried. "The set pieces are all different. I think we changed every move, every entrance and exit."

"Gretchen's an overly-eager-to-please sophomore, and Joe's a perfectionist. They wrote it all down. They'll remember."

"Why are you so smart all of a sudden?"

Faith tipped her face up to the rain and laughed. "I don't know!" She had no idea where her sudden nerve was coming from, either.

Suddenly Christopher crossed in front of her, grabbing her in a mock tackle so that there was no alternative but to grab him around the waist, too. He almost slipped, then clutched her even more tightly, one hand sliding up her back and the other winding around her hip.

In spite of the cool rain, Faith was warm inside. For a moment they stood there, staring at each other. Touching. Faith told herself not to read too much into it. Christopher always encouraged, rewarded, and sympathized with his cast and crew through pats on the back, quick hugs, and a hand on the shoulder. Touching was just his way.

Faith swallowed hard, because Christopher wasn't

taking his hands away. The longer he held her, the more wobbly and aware of his touch she became. Neither of them said anything, and Faith wondered if she would ever think of anything to say ever again.

Then a flap of wind blew big droplets of water off a nearby tree.

"You have mud on your shoes," she whispered.

"I do?"

"I've never seen you looking anything less than perfect before."

"Can you take it?"

"I guess so."

He ran his palm down the side of her face.

Faith looked away. Maybe she *couldn't* take it. She was too tired to fight the wooziness. "Do you know that when I first met you, Merideth called you 'Sir Christopher'?"

"Figures." He shook his head.

"Does it?"

"Some people have a pretty overinflated idea of who I am."

"Like who?"

He pulled his hands away, intentionally. "Never mind." He took a step back and looked over his shoulder, toward the center of campus. "You know, I've got class."

"Yeah," Faith joked. "I knew you had some-thing."

"Very funny," Christopher groaned. He stuck his hands in his pockets and took in every inch of her again. "Sometimes I get the feeling that maybe you *are* just an overeager freshman. And then other times I feel like you're one of the few people in the world who might really know me. The real me. Not Sir Christopher, but the junior who's doing too many things at one time, so he doesn't quite give any of them his all."

Faith wasn't quite sure what he was talking about, but she loved the fervent way he looked at her. Water dribbled down her face and inside her suede jacket, and still she might have stood there forever if Christopher hadn't abruptly turned away and said, "See you tonight, Faith. See you tonight."

After he was gone, Faith walked, head down, slipping, still awkward and out of control. She wasn't quite sure what had just happened; all she knew was that it was another first—another strange, scary, out-of-this-world first.

But as she neared her dorm, she made herself think about earthly things. She'd missed her language-lab appointment that morning—she hoped she could sneak in over the weekend. The only class she had was Stagecraft 2, then rehearsal that night—where she would see Christopher again. But if she didn't get some sleep she'd probably turn into a jelly-brained nut case who might faint or attack him in front of everyone.

The only thing she could see really clearly was that she needed to get some rest that afternoon. But her dorm was always so noisy. All day long there was always someone singing, reciting, or dropping juggling balls. The only places on campus less conducive to sleep would have been Winnie's party dorm or the parking lot where they were steamrolling new asphalt.

"Langston House," Faith reminded herself, changing direction and picking up speed.

KC's dorm had a twenty-four-hour quiet rule. And from what Faith could remember, KC had an accounting class and her business discussion group that afternoon. Her room would be the perfect place to crash for at least a few hours.

The rain started to let up, so that by the time Faith arrived at Langston House, she looked only half-drenched. KC was on her way out of her room. There was a strange, totally distracted look in her gray eyes and she nearly smacked into Faith as they met in the doorway.

"Hi," Faith greeted happily.

"What?" KC looked so alarmed that Faith almost expected to see someone stowed away under her bed. But KC's tiny single room was empty. Just her narrow bed, the desk, and the bare walls. Not a single memento, postcard, or reminder of home. "I just got here, and I have to leave again. I have a quiz," she rambled.

"Okay. I just wanted to ask if I could take a nap here this afternoon," Faith asked, starting to bubble over in a frothy giggle again. "I was up all night with Christopher."

KC's gray eyes hardened with shock.

"I don't mean *that,*" Faith came back playfully. She tried to tickle KC, but it was like grabbing a hunk of iron. "We were working the whole time. It was great."

KC stood in the doorway to her room, barely moving, her perfect face a block of solid distress.

"Can I nap here? KC? Are you in there? You haven't been taken over by aliens since I last saw you, have you? Alien accountants from the planet Soccer Shirt . . ."

"Faith, stop!" KC exploded, reacting with surprising rage.

Faith's sleepy giddiness flattened out. "I'm sorry, KC. What's the matter? What's going on?"

"More than you know," KC snapped. "I have to tell you . . . a lot of things. I have to—oh, God. I'm late for class."

Faith stayed in the doorway while KC ran down the stairs. But after that she was too tired to worry. She pulled off her boots, dropped onto KC's single bed, and fell fast asleep.

Twelve

As soon as KC sat down in her business discussion group on Tuesday morning, she was face-to-face with Steven Garth.

"Little angel," he said, flopping over her desk and leaning on his elbows. "I missed you. It's only been a few days, but I missed you anyway."

KC couldn't look at him. She felt as if a lifetime had passed since she'd seen him last.

He inched closer, then reached out and stroked her cheek. "Oh, no, Angeletti. I thought we were getting somewhere. Don't tell me I have to start all over again at square one." Even though he was teasing, it was friendly teasing. The barbs were gone.

"What?" KC didn't know what to make of his

sudden warmth. Especially considering the mess she was in. "What do you mean?"

He rolled his eyes, then took her hand. "What do I mean? What happened, little angel? Did you lose your memory or something? Is that the effect I have on you?"

"You have no effect on me," KC came back.

"So how come your hand is shaking?"

KC tried to keep her hand still. "It's not."

"Oh, yeah?"

She stared as he took out a pen and scribbled on her trembling palm, *Hi, partner. We make a great team.*

KC was afraid she might start to cry. She was saved only by Naomi calling the class to order. But soon Steven was in KC's face again, as they gathered with Helen and Edward and KC had to begin her sales report.

"So, well, that makes four hundred and eighty dollars, which I, uh, yes, I deposited this morning." She tried to sound professional even though she felt like she wanted to bolt out of the room. "But I think we can keep taking orders for another week and still be able to, uh, get the shirts in time for the first game." She glanced at Steven, ready for another challenge.

"Which isn't for three weeks," he added. "So I think we can keep taking orders for another few days." After offering his comment he folded his hands and sat back in his desk chair.

"Uh, thank you, Steven."

Steven was now Mr. Polite and Subdued. Although he stared at KC, there was something friendly in his eyes. KC immediately became paranoid. Was he being nice to her because he somehow knew she was in trouble?

Steven was still staring at her, playing with the clasp on his Rolex, as if he expected her to go on. But KC had lost her nerve. She shuffled and reshuffled her papers. *Why doesn't somebody else take some responsibility for this project?* she asked herself. *Why do Helen and Edward just sit there like blocks of stone?*

Steven took over. "So, Helen, we won't need your help until the shirts are ready. And Edward, we should probably make up another set of flyers to pump up these last few days of sales."

Helen and Edward were entranced, visions of *A*s and dollars undoubtedly dancing in their heads.

Visions of disaster kept running through KC's head, though.

"KC, do you want to add anything?"

"Nothing." KC's answer came out like a wet, sopping towel that she had just thrown over Steven's head. He looked surprised, but let it go by. There was more talk about how they would do their written report, about setting up an inventory and bookkeeping system when the shirts came in. KC sank down in her desk chair as if it were a foxhole. She wished that the clock on the wall would speed up. When the four of them decided to break early, she scrambled out of her seat.

KC flew out of the room like a tornado. Everything about her felt like a lie. Her jacket, her shoes, her stupid calculator, her success—all of it felt like a lie. She wondered how long she could hide the fact that she'd stolen from her own business. She prayed she could somehow make up the money before Steven and the others found out.

Steven caught her in the hall.

"What?" She pulled away from him.

"What," he mimicked. "What do you think? That I want to mug you? Please go into the men's room with me so I can steal your wallet." When she didn't laugh, he said, "I just want to talk to you. Is that allowed?"

She could hardly say, *No, go away, don't ever lay eyes on me again*. After all, he was her classmate, her partner. She stared down at her shoes while he pulled her down the hall and out onto the landing of the concrete stairs.

"You are one strange girl," he said, shaking his head. The rain had long since cleared and there was a clean breeze. Steven's shaggy hair fluttered as he brushed it away from his eyes.

"Look who's talking."

"I guess I'd better make this short," he decided. "I can tell you're not in a real receptive mood."

"Do you know what I can tell?" she ranted. "You think because you're Steven Garth, of Garth Petroleum, that I'm drooling over you every second, that I can hardly stop myself from jumping your bones."

"I did hope—"

KC turned away, grabbing the handrail. She wasn't sure where the part about drooling over Steven had come from, and she wished she could take it back. But it was all connected in some horrible way. Steven. Money. Courtney. Lauren. Buzz Off. Business class and the stupid Tri Betas.

"Come on, Angeletti. I admit I started this, but I thought we were getting past it."

"Wait a minute!" KC whirled around. "You said *I* started it. When we went to Bernhard's, you said I was the one who started it."

Finally, that mocking grin came back. "I'll try anything. What can I say?"

"You would try anything, wouldn't you?" KC started down the steps, but he caught her wrist and held on hard. "Ow." She turned back.

"So how about going out to dinner tonight?"

"What?"

"You know. Go out, eat. Food. You don't even have to talk to me if you don't want to. You can throw your drink at me, stomp on my toes under the table. We'll have a great time.''

"I can't."

"Why? It's Friday night."

"I just can't."

"That's not a reason."

"Fine!" she shouted. "All right! I'll meet you. Anywhere you want! Just leave me alone!"

"Okay. See you tonight, then. Seven o'clock. The Blue Whale."

KC wrenched her arm away from him, and when she was sure he could no longer see her, she began to sob.

Going . . . going . . . gone.

Winnie's eyelids were going down for the count. Her handwriting had turned into a squiggly blur and she was starting to tilt and totter over her desk.

"The period between the mid-twelfth and the mid-fifteenth centuries served as a transitional stage from Kievan to Muscovite Russia. The dilemma of the Mongol invasion . . . "

Dilemma. Winnie knew a dilemma when she saw one. Right then it was how to stay awake in honors history. And how to keep her mind on track, following the lecture on the Mongol hordes, not drifting back to the night before.

But last night had been so . . . mind boggling. The

Zero Bagel stayed open until three, and that's just how late she'd hung out with Josh. They'd played pool, eaten the truly terrible goulash, talked about how they both dreamed of a trip around the world. When they'd finally returned to Forest Hall, Josh had kissed her cheek and said goodnight as if nothing more had ever happened between them. It had certainly been better than avoiding Josh, feeling like a reject and a fool. But it was still too bizarre really to comprehend.

Winnie told herself to tune back into the lecture. She kept drifting off, then coming to again with a jolt, as if she'd run into an electric fence.

"Part of the reason for Moscow's rise was geographic. Lying on the Moskva River . . ."

Winnie watched her professor's mouth move. His name was Dr. Karp and he was a short block of a man who wore the kind of short-sleeved shirts that Winnie associated with dentists. Her focus zoomed in and out. The map hung over the board seemed to be moving. Her pen seemed to be attached to someone else's hand. Her other palm slid along the side of her face and she had to lower her head, just for one short, split second. . . .

The lecture was over.

Backpacks were being zipped up. Sweaters were pulled on. Desks were shoved aside. Dr. Karp was no longer behind his lectern, but was chatting with a student in the middle of the room.

Winnie looked at the clock. She'd slept through the last twenty minutes of class! She felt dazed and fuzzy. People were filing out. Closing her notebook, she stuck it into her Barbie-doll bag, preparing to leave, too.

As soon as she stood up, Dr. Karp called out, "Ms. Gottlieb."

Winnie froze.

He waited until all the other students were gone. While Winnie stood at attention by her desk, he erased his outline from the board.

"Are you well, Ms. Gottlieb?" he asked.

"What?"

He turned around and collected his notes. His goatee was gray and he had sparkly eyes with deep creases underneath. "If you're ill, I suggest you stay home and not infect the rest of us. If you're just tired, I suggest you sleep at night. You transferred into this class late, so you're already playing catch-up. Don't make it any harder on yourself."

"I'm sorry," Winnie mumbled. "I know."

Dr. Karp wasn't very interested in her reply. He snapped his lecture notes into his briefcase, nodded curtly, then held the door open until she'd shuffled out of the room.

* * *

Knock. Knock. Knock.

"KC? Are you home?"

That voice was echoing deep inside Faith's memory, welling up from some bygone dreamy place. The face that went with it filled her head, too, making her feel safe, as if she were surrounded by her folks and her sister, Marlee, and her old high-school friends, her old room, her old school, her old life.

Knock. Knock.

"KC?"

Faith barely lifted her head from KC's pillow. She tried to open her eyes, but she didn't want to break the dream. She was at her high-school prom dancing with Christopher, wearing the vest she'd borrowed on top of her first formal dress, a pink satin thing her mother had bought for her when she was only fifteen. Christopher moved slowly, without his usual slick grace. His arms were surprisingly protective and secure. He wasn't someone who had a hug for everyone. His touch was only for her.

Snuggling down under the blankets, Faith had a vague sense that Christopher's hair had changed, too. It was longish and curly, and his face looked younger, less defined. She wondered why he had ever reminded her of a newscaster or a politician, because he wasn't like that at all. No. He was a jock. And an outdoorsman. A handsome, sure-minded, small-town boy. The kind of guy you could trust with anything, who'd never lie to you or let you down.

"KC?"

Faith wanted so badly to stay in the dreamy fog. To dance and sway, to let images rush and fade. Coming out was like climbing out of a pit. It took too much effort, and she sank back into the dream again until her eyes really focused and the dream was replaced by something joltingly real.

"Faith?"

"Brooks?"

"What are you doing in here? Where's KC?"

Brooks was standing in front of her, wearing one of KC's sample soccer shirts. For a moment Faith had no idea where she was. Back home in Jacksonville? Waking up after a high-school slumber party?

"A nap. I needed a nap." Faith wondered what time it was.

Brooks looked disoriented, too. He held onto the doorknob as if he were going to recheck the room number. "The door was unlocked. I just wanted to leave some more orders for her. I didn't know . . . "

"That I was here?" Faith rubbed her face. She was still wearing the same clothes she'd worn all day yesterday and the night before. Her mouth felt like moldy cotton.

Brooks stammered, "If I'd known . . ."

"You never would have come in."

Anger flashed across his familiar face. It was a look Faith remembered from the time he'd lost his footing while practicing rock climbing the week before.

"What's wrong with your own room?"

"It's just noisy. Too noisy. That's all."

"Why are you so tired? How long have you been asleep?"

Finally Faith was one hundred percent awake. Everything had come back to her, including the fact that Brooks wasn't speaking to her and she wasn't speaking to him. That they'd arrived at college as a pair, and now they were separate as foes.

"What business is it of yours?" she accused. "I thought you never wanted to talk to me again. So how come now it's twenty questions?" She flopped back down on KC's bed. "What time is it? I want to go back to sleep."

He came further into the room and took KC's desk chair and turned it around, so he could sit with his arms on the backrest. He glared at Faith with suspicious eyes. "It's almost five. You'd better get up. You're going to miss dinner."

Faith realized that she was starving, that she'd missed her stagecraft class, and that she only had two hours before rehearsal. That meant two hours to shower and change, eat, and get her foggy brain together. She sat up and found her cowboy boots. "I have to get ready for rehearsal."

"Right," Brooks said with a sarcasm Faith had never heard in high school. "You're working with that frat guy, Christopher Hammond. Well, I wouldn't get too carried away over him if I were you, because from what I've heard he's engaged to some girl from another school."

Everything in Faith's head went gray and mushy again. Christopher was engaged? To be married? It wasn't possible. "He is not."

Brooks seemed to take her denial as a confession of guilt. "Oh, yes he is. I asked a guy in my dorm who's pledging the same fraternity. So if he's the reason you broke up with me, you should know that he has a fiancée."

Faith threw back the blankets. She didn't know if she'd ever been as angry as she was at that moment. "Christopher had nothing to do with breaking up with you! And I—I don't care if he has a fiancée. All I'm doing is assisting him on a musical. I'm a theater-arts major. I'm getting three credits. What's it to you?"

"I'm sorry, Faith," he said sadly, standing up and backing toward the door. "Look, I didn't come here trying to find you. I'm not ready to see you. I'm not ready to deal with any of this yet. All I know is Christopher Hammond is engaged and if anything's going on between the two of you, then you should know."

"Thanks a lot," Faith muttered. "Now would you

please leave? This is a girls-only dorm. For all I know, you're not even supposed to be in here."

"I'm going," he swore, tossing down an envelope meant for KC. "Believe me, I don't want to hang around here any longer."

Faith stared at her boots, not moving, barely breathing, until she'd convinced herself that what Brooks had told her couldn't possibly be true.

Thirteen

·····································

I'm going to be late. I know it. Oh, this is perfect. Perfect!"

Lauren was hustling, moving fast, even though her low heels dug little dents into the damp earth. She was taking a shortcut across the athletic fields as dusk fell, heading back into campus from Sorority Row.

"Thanks again, Marielle," she muttered. "Thank you so much."

Lauren had finished her "Dorm Life" article that afternoon, making her deadline with hours to spare. But had she been able to find a free fifteen minutes to take it over to the newspaper office? No. Her Latin teacher had kept her overtime. She'd gotten held up in the world's slowest line at the student store. And finally she'd had to meet Marielle at the Tri Beta house to look through fashion magazines and hear a lecture on dark colors and wide belts.

"I should just tell her to take her dark colors and . . . oh, I don't know," Lauren grumbled, knowing she would never tell Marielle much of anything. After all, without the Tri Beta sorority, what did she have at U of S? KC? Her great friends in Rapids Hall? Since classes had begun, even Faith and Winnie barely had time for her.

"Just hurry," she ordered herself, even though she was breathless and a stitch was pulling on her side. "Hurry!"

Lauren had put her last, desperate hopes in the newspaper, but how late would their office stay open? It was nearly six o'clock. On Fridays, Dash probably left at three. She was bound to race over there only to be greeted by a dark room, locked doors, and no way to prove that she had indeed completed her assignment on time.

The campus was emptying out. There were vacant spaces in the parking lots and the bookstore had already closed. So had the admissions office and the health center.

By the time Lauren reached the journalism building, almost all the daylight was gone, and so was her hope. She was surprised to find the main doors unlocked, but once inside, she found the first floor as deserted as she thought it would be. The only people she saw before rushing downstairs were a janitor and some professor changing notices in a display case.

Her heels echoed in the hallway as Lauren trotted down to the basement. She considered tacking her article to the door or trying to find Dash Ramirez's home phone number, except that she knew she'd never have the nerve to do either of those things. She'd simply chalk it up as one more failure and limp back to the dorm.

But as soon as Lauren dropped down off the last step, she was assaulted by a rush of frantic activity and noise. Keyboards clacking. Voices. Footsteps. Doors slamming. Banks of fluorescent lights giving off a harsh, white glare.

The door to *The Journal* was propped open with a stack of newspapers. Unlike the first time Lauren had visited the office, the place was unbelievably crowded. It reminded Lauren of an ant farm; there were so many students busily scurrying around the aisles and between chairs. Dash was at his desk, surrounded by a mess of papers. His computer was on and he was comparing a page in his hand with the text up on the screen.

Lauren waited for students to clear the entrance, then moved awkwardly in front of his desk, pulling out her copy of "Dorm Life" and her fountain pen.

When Dash finally looked up at her, she wondered

if he remembered who she was. He had on a tight-fitting black T-shirt, with the same bandanna around his forehead and what could have been the same cigarette hanging out of the corner of his mouth.

"Excuse me," she managed.

"What?"

"Excuse me."

"Speak up. I can barely hear you. You want to whisper, go to the library."

Lauren placed her article on the one clean corner of his desk. "You assigned me a tryout article for the homecoming supplement. Remember? Dorm life. Well, here's my piece."

Recollection flashed across his brown eyes. He took one last puff, then flipped his cigarette into a used Styrofoam coffee cup. "You came through. What do you know." He quickly looked over her pages, nodding in approval at her neatly printed computer type. Then he went back to his own screen.

Lauren figured she was supposed to make an about-face and disappear, but she couldn't do it. Her legs were too tired, and she wasn't ready to face the dorm just yet. Besides, she'd put a lot into her article. After throwing out her drecky first drafts, she'd found a real angle. The final version was quirky, funny but sad. It was too personal just to slap it on Dash Ramirez's desk with no more fanfare than a parking ticket.

"I was afraid everyone would be gone," she admitted.

"Huh?"

"That I would miss you. That the office would be closed."

He looked up at her with disbelief. "Don't I wish. We'll be here until ten at least. We have to get out a camera-ready copy of the next issue by tomorrow."

Lauren just kept standing there, rocking on her good, sensible shoes, clutching her bag, until finally she picked up her article again, took out her pen and scratched her dorm address and hall phone number on the front page. "Will you at least write me a note and let me know what you think of it?"

"Sure." He was watching her, his eyes narrowing. "Nice pen."

Dash's gaze made her so nervous that she heard herself say, "Do you want it?" She held out the fountain pen.

Now he was looking at her as if she'd just asked him to take a pleasure cruise to the North Pole. "No. I don't want it." He shook his head and readjusted his bandanna, then picked up her article and began to look it over.

Lauren felt like an idiot. What did she expect? That if she gave him her expensive fountain pen, he'd like her article? Was she going to trade her CD player for a kind word? Her BMW for a best friend? Those girls in her dorm were right. She *was* pathetic.

Lauren started to back out, but Dash was still reading. Unlike the first time, when he'd skimmed so furiously, he was actually going back to the beginning and reading the whole piece again. There was the hint of a smile on his face. And then Lauren heard an amazing sound. She heard it over the clacking of keyboards, over the footsteps and the buzz of the fluorescent lights and the busy talk. Dash chuckled.

He gestured for her to come closer.

"Yes?"

"This isn't bad." He paused to check her name on the article. "Lauren. I didn't think anybody could do much with 'Dorm Life.' "

"You really like it?"

He read it over another time, rubbing his five o'clock shadow and chuckling some more. "Funny stuff."

Now Lauren was practically bouncing up and down.

"I'll show it to the editor. Don't get your hopes up—I mean as far as getting it printed. But I'm sure he'll be interested in seeing more."

Lauren stood at his desk, beaming and bouncing, until she realized that she probably looked like a moron. Still, she waited for something else from Dash. *A goodbye, good work, good luck.* But his eyes were glued to his computer screen again, so Lauren made her way back through the busy crowd and out the door.

Suddenly she couldn't wait to get back to the dorm. Not that there was anyone waiting for her there, but at least she felt like she had something to offer this campus, some way to fit in. Actually, it made her want to get to know this rugged Western place more deeply. She wanted to think, to go for a drive. Maybe even cruise up into the steep nearby mountains, get past the snow line and look down over the town of Springfield, the college, the dorms, to get a better perspective on her life.

Some things were starting to come together in Lauren's head as she strode across the green. Until now she'd felt material things were all she had to give to people. But she had finally realized it was better to be the oddball person she really was rather than some overly polite, eternally generous society blob.

The usual ambitious artsiness greeted her back at Coleridge. Modern dancers were rehearsing in the lobby. Someone had an easel set up near the RA's room, and she could smell photo-developing chemicals as she passed the bathroom on the first floor.

The door to her dorm room was open and she was glad to see that Faith was home. She suddenly wanted to tell Faith everything: how out of place she felt with the Tri Betas, how strange things were with KC, how she knew she'd made the mistake of giving too much.

But Faith was on her way out the door, already wearing her fringed jacket and chomping on a slab of bread and peanut butter. Her usual serenity had been replaced by a harried nervousness.

"KC came by and took your car keys," Faith explained as she made sure she had her room key. "She said she had to go down to The Blue Whale. Maybe they have an opening for a waitress or a coat-check girl or something. I'm not sure." She checked the clock. "I've got to go to rehearsal. See you later."

"Bye," Lauren whispered. All the joy and hope had leaked out of her. She collapsed on her bed.

When she had offered the use of her BMW to KC, she'd expected to be treated considerately, as a friend. But KC would barely give her the time of day, and still she had come by and taken Lauren's car without asking.

"I *am* pathetic!"

Maybe it was time to do something. Anything was better than being talked about behind her back, buying her way into a sorority, trying to bribe someone into liking her article with a stupid fountain pen.

"Just do it," she told herself. "Don't wait until you've calmed down. Do it now while you have the nerve to tell her what's on your mind."

Lauren went to the hall phone, called Mountain Taxi, and asked them to pick her up right away and give her a ride down to The Blue Whale.

* * *

"Who are you, anyway?"

"What do you mean, who am I?"

"Who are you? Where do you live? In some mansion somewhere? How do I know you didn't make the whole Garth Petroleum thing up? Since the time we almost ran into each other in the parking lot, I haven't seen you around the dorms."

"I have a dorm room, little angel. But most of the time I stay in a condo downtown. My dad keeps it for business."

"Where? Right off The Strand, probably."

"Not far off."

KC sat across from Steven Garth, candles and crystal goblets between them. She'd thought of standing Steven up, but she hadn't been able to stay away. She'd wanted to tell him off, but she hadn't succeeded in that, either. Part of her never wanted to see Steven Garth again. And another part of her couldn't stop thinking about him.

So she sat tall at The Blue Whale, a filet of grilled halibut getting cold on the plate in front of her. She hadn't touched a bite. Instead she'd filled her mouth with questions. Since she didn't seem to be able to stay away from Steven, at least she could steer the conversation away from soccer shirts and bank deposits.

Meanwhile, he ate slowly, watching her with his searing eyes.

"So why do you go to U of S? If you're so rich, Steven Garth, how come you don't go to Harvard or Yale or some other fancy private school?"

He shrugged, digging into his lobster with considerable skill and ease. "I couldn't get in. I'm not a brilliant student, like you are."

KC didn't think of herself as brilliant. She just tried harder. "I'm okay. But why couldn't you get into one of those schools anyway? I'm sure you had great connections."

"I'm from around here. I like the West. I didn't want to have to work that hard." He offered her a taste of lobster, which she declined. "Partner, let me ask you a question or two."

KC steeled herself.

"Aren't you hungry?"

She didn't answer.

"You're not one of those girls who doesn't eat in public, are you?"

"Of course not."

"I'm paying."

"No, you're not."

"Okay, I'm not." He laughed. "In that case, I'll have dessert."

The dinner looked even less appealing. There was no way KC could pick up the check, so she could only hope that once the tab arrived they would bicker over it again, and she could let Steven win. But then she saw something that made her more uneasy than the check, almost as uneasy as the Soccer, Inc. bank account. It was Lauren, leaning toward the maitre d' and looking around the restaurant.

KC told herself that it was only a coincidence, that Lauren was meeting someone from the sorority. But then Lauren spotted her and walked right over.

"Hello," Lauren whispered.

"Hi. This is Steven Garth," KC said, making the introductions with utter politeness. She still told herself not to freak out. Knowing Lauren, she would probably offer to pay for their dinner herself. KC just prayed that Lauren wouldn't inadvertently say the wrong thing. "Steven, this is Lauren Turnbell-Smythe. Lauren rooms with one of my best friends from high school."

"Nice to know you have best friends, Angeletti," he quipped. "I was beginning to worry."

KC was trying to think of a comeback when she heard a scary new urgency in Lauren's voice.

"I'm sorry to bother you," Lauren was saying. "I didn't know that you were dining here, KC. Faith thought you'd come down to look for a job. But, um, I need my car and you didn't ask if you could use it, and now I see you have another way to get home, so I really feel that I should ask you to give back the keys."

KC could feel Steven's eyes hone in on her like the lens of a camera. He pushed his dinner aside and folded his arms.

Unable to speak, KC dug in her purse for Lauren's car keys.

"The starving-student special?" Steven wanted to know. "The white Beamer is yours?"

Lauren nodded, then turned back to KC. "I really am sorry to interrupt your dinner, but I had to do this." She took the keys from KC and backed away. "I won't disturb you anymore. I'm sorry. We can talk back at the dorm."

After Lauren left, Steven stared at KC with his cocky smile. "So, partner," he needled. "You want to tell me what's going on?"

KC pushed her plate clear across the table. She shoved back her chair and, almost smacking into the dessert cart, ran out of The Blue Whale and onto The Strand.

Fourteen

··

Winnie, you have a visitor," said Melissa. Winnie lifted her face out of her history book. She'd caught up on the first two chapters in *Russia and the Soviet Union* and gotten a start on her French homework, but she still had two more history chapters to read that weekend, plus she had to start *The Odyssey* for Western Civ and find some time to watch a video of an ancient Hitchcock movie she'd missed during the first week of film class.

"Winnie."

"Oh. Hi, Josh."

"What's going on?" Josh stuck his hands in his pockets as he noticed Melissa, who was at her desk in blue spandex running tights and a hooded sweatshirt.

"Oh. Josh, this is Melissa McDormand, my room-mate. Melissa, this is Josh."

"Hi, Melissa. How's it going?"

"Howdy." Melissa lifted her head briefly, smiled, then went back to her homework.

Josh fingered his earring, staring at Melissa with a puzzled expression. "Melissa, I haven't met you, have I? With all the parties in this dorm, I thought I'd met most everybody who lived on our floor."

"Not me." Melissa suddenly closed her book, as if she'd decided that Josh's presence would make fur-ther study impossible. She traded her homework for her plastic basket containing shampoo, soap, towel, and rubber thongs. "I don't party much," she said pleasantly as she headed out the door. "I'm pre-med."

Josh nodded. "That explains it. My roommate's pre-med and I never see him, either. Nice to meet you."

"You, too. See you later." Melissa gave Winnie half a smile, then left her alone with Josh.

Someone down the hall was blasting their stereo again and Winnie felt the vibrations through her bed. Josh flopped down next to her. For a while they both smiled at each other and bobbed to the beat.

"That was fun the other night, at The Zero Ba-gel," Josh finally said.

"Yeah. It was."

He leaned across her to check out the cover of her book. "Pretty interesting?"

"Some of it. Those early Slavs are hard to beat when it comes to excitement."

He laughed.

"It's kind of hard to keep my concentration going," Winnie admitted. "Unlike Melissa, I can be distracted by just about anything. My clock ticking. A fly. The veins on those anatomy models."

He nudged her. "Good thing you're not premed."

"Really." Winnie put her book away. She liked having Josh sitting in her room in such a friendly, casual way. And she liked the fact that *he* had made the effort to come find *her*, not the other way around. "Anything new in your classes?"

"I had my first test this afternoon. In my engineering class. I was up half of last night studying, but I think I aced it." He reached back and pulled a folded copy of *The Journal* from the back pocket of his jeans. "So do you have some big date tonight, or should we find the worst movie in town and go see it? How about *Killer Bimbos from Planet X*?"

"*Killer Bimbos from Planet X*? I don't believe it."

"That's what it says right here."

"What do you know. It does say that. I bet it's a classic."

"Undoubtedly."

"It'll probably be my next assignment for film class."

"It will. Trace the symbolism lines down the monsters' backs. Do they stand for the spinelessness of alien life, or did they just forget to hide the zippers on the monster costumes?"

They laughed.

Josh popped up and held his arms out for Winnie. "Come on."

Winnie jumped up, too. She was grinning. She liked the idea of starting again with Josh.

"Let's go downtown," he wooed. "If we decide to skip the movie, we'll find something to do. Bowling. Miniature golf. We can go to the bus station and pretend we're taking a trip to Klamath Falls."

Winnie liked the idea that Josh was pursuing her, that for once in her life she was being fairly cool and restrained. The only thing she didn't like was the thought of Dr. Karp's scowl or another lecture from Mr. Morain.

"Thanks, I'd really like to," she heard herself say. "And I know it's Friday night and all, but I transferred into two classes late, plus I've got my other homework. I feel like if I don't catch up and nail it this weekend, I'll be behind for the rest of my life. So I think I'll take a rain check. Or a bowling check. How does that sound?"

Josh looked surprised and disappointed. But he didn't look like he was going to give up.

"I understand," he said. "How about if we plan something for next weekend? We could figure it out ahead of time and then you could plan your homework around that."

Winnie wanted to jump up and kiss Josh. But she didn't. Instead, she led Josh to the door.

"That sounds great," she told him. "That sounds just great."

Faith's heart was pounding.

"If it weren't for you, it never would have gone so well," Christopher was telling her later that same Friday evening. "Never."

"That's not true."

"Oh, yes it is. If it weren't for you, that woman from the station would never have been so impressed. I'm going to get that internship, Faith. I can feel it. I'm going to get it."

"I hope you're right."

"I am. And it's all due to you, Faith. All the credit is yours."

They were in a small back booth at Toole's Tavern. The rest of the *Stop the World* company hung out at Luigi's, but Christopher had wanted to take Faith to Toole's, a dark, smoky establishment with framed photos on the walls and the echoey twang of jazz guitar. Toole's wasn't a dorm hangout. It wasn't a fraternity hangout. Actually, Faith didn't recognize anyone there, which was fortunate since she'd ordered a glass of wine and was three years away from the legal drinking age.

Christopher, who was twenty-one, sipped a frothy beer and gazed at her across the table. A candle sputtered between them. "You really are an extraordinary girl."

"No, I'm not. I'm just glad I could help."

"Oh, you've helped, Faith. You've helped a lot of things in my life since we started working together."

Faith wasn't sure how to respond, or even quite what Christopher was trying to say. The golden warmth in his voice was making her woozy. She didn't trust that it was really happening, or that she could let herself get carried away with this lush, dangerous feeling.

"Don't you have someone waiting for you this weekend?" she hinted.

Christopher stared into his beer. "Nope. How about you?"

"No."

"Nobody?"

Faith shook her head. "Not anymore."

They listened to the guitarist again like they were both jazz experts, leaning over the table and staring at anything but each other. Faith tried to drink the rest of her wine, but it tasted strange and even a few sips had made her feel lightheaded.

Finally Christopher said, "It's late. Let's go."

"Okay." Dragging her fringed jacket behind her, Faith followed Christopher out of the bar.

Christopher drove a sporty two-person coupe with a dashboard that gleamed. He held the door open for her, then locked her in. For one short second she was alone with the rough pounding of her heart.

Then he was next to her again. He put the key in the ignition, but instead of starting the car he leaned forward over the steering wheel and stared up at the dark sky. Faith sat close to him, feeling like they were enclosed in the same bubble.

Still Christopher didn't start the car. There seemed to be a dozen silent conversations crisscrossing between them as another car pulled out of the lot and shot its headlights across their faces. Finally Christopher reached for the gear shift. Then he reached past it. Faith turned at the same time he reached for her and—it was happening. They were kissing. His hands were on her face, her back, her hair. She was reaching frantically for him, too, not thinking or holding back, letting something new, something crazy take over inside her.

She wanted to say, *What about your fiancée? Tell me it's not true, that you're not engaged, that she doesn't exist. Tell me it was something that Brooks made up to hurt me*. But she didn't ask. She didn't demand. She didn't accuse. Because down deep, Faith knew that Christopher could be engaged to a dozen other girls—and it still wouldn't make a bit of difference.

Fifteen

hen KC knocked on Faith and Lauren's door it was late. KC was cold. Her feet hurt. Though she'd come to see Lauren, as soon as she walked in she asked, "Where's Faith?"

Lauren was sitting at her computer wearing wire-rimmed glasses and a flannel nightgown. For once she looked as sloppy as any other dorm freshman.

"She's not here. Her rehearsal must have gone really late."

KC looked over at Faith's side of the room. Faith was usually neat and organized, but that night she'd left paint-dotted overalls, scripts, tights, and papers strewn about. "It's after midnight."

Lauren stared.

KC closed the door. She hadn't wanted to do this, but on her long, horrible walk back from The Blue Whale, she'd decided this was the only way. "Lauren, I'm sorry if I didn't ask to use your car. I thought you told me I could borrow it when I needed to—"

Lauren interrupted, "When you needed to look for a job! That's what I said. But KC, you weren't looking for a job tonight."

"No. I was on a date."

"Didn't you assume I'd want you to *ask* before you took my car? Didn't you assume I'd ever need it?"

"Didn't *you* assume I didn't want you coming up and embarrassing me in the middle of a date?" KC retorted.

Lauren tensed. "I'm sorry if I embarrassed you in front of your date. I just got so angry when I came back here and . . ." Lauren stood up and clenched her fists. "I thought we were friends, KC. But it hasn't felt very friendly since classes began."

A sob caught in KC's throat. After everything that had happened over the last few days, she didn't have much resistance left.

"All I want is for us to be friends, KC."

Suddenly a light went on in KC's head. If Lauren really wanted to be her friend, maybe she would help. "Lauren, maybe you could do me a huge favor, as a friend."

"What?"

KC took a deep, hard breath. "It has to do with my business class."

"Yes?"

"I owe some money. I know I'll get another job really soon and be able to pay everything back. But in the meantime, I owe a few hundred dollars or so."

"What do you want from me?"

KC cleared her throat. It was difficult to get the words out. "I was wondering if you could, well, give me a loan. I don't expect it to be like the dress. I mean a real loan, where I'll pay you back as soon as I get another job."

Lauren hesitated for a moment, and then her face hardened. There was a new strength in her round violet eyes. "I can't," she said.

"What?"

"I'm sorry, KC. I can't."

"Lauren, I'm in trouble! There's no one else I can go to. Faith and Winnie don't have extra spending money."

"What about the guy you were with at dinner?" Lauren demanded. "If he can afford to take you to The Blue Whale, he can probably afford to loan you a few hundred dollars."

How could KC explain that the whole point of borrowing was to avoid getting caught by Steven? All her anger was rushing back. At the Tri Betas, at Steven, at her parents for being such flaky fools. "Lauren, I lost my job because of you. What kind of a friend are you that you won't even pay me back?"

Lauren's eyes filled with tears. "What kind of friend are you to put me in this position? All I am is generous with my so-called friends, and all they do is take advantage of me!"

"Thanks a lot," KC said. "I never should have asked you."

"KC!" Lauren objected.

But KC didn't hear anything else because she ran out, slamming the door behind her. She flew downstairs, past some dancers rehearsing in the Coleridge lobby. Her heart was still pounding long after she'd raced across the green and back to Langston Hall.

But before she could get behind the safety of her girls-only front door, a pair of arms grabbed her and pulled her back onto the muddy green.

"What do you want from me?" she heaved.

Steven's hair flopped over his forehead. His smile was gone and his eyes were more insistent than ever. He grabbed her arms and made her look at him. "I've been waiting for you all night. I want you to tell me what's going on, partner."

KC tried to get away from him. "What do you mean?"

"I mean, like why you pretended you owned that Beamer. Where's your car? In the shop?"

"I don't have a car," KC spat back. "I never said I did."

Steven pulled her closer. "You never said you didn't. What else haven't you told me?"

"Nothing!"

"Why did you want me to think you drove a BMW?"

KC felt the clutch of tears again. "Why do you think?"

"You wanted to impress me? God, Angeletti, why didn't you tell me that when we first met? All I've been doing this whole time is trying to get your attention."

KC twisted away from him and fled across the lawn. But he caught up with her, grabbing her again and pulling her down. They tumbled onto the spongy, cold grass. Steven held KC so closely that she could barely move.

"So what's the truth, Angeletti?" he panted. "Are you really an orphan? Do you have two ugly stepsisters who make you scrub the floors? Were you switched at birth for Princess Diana?"

"I'm not anything," she ranted, tears pouring down her face. "I'm not rich, I'm not poor. I'm just normal, average, able to scrape by—just barely—and I work ten times harder than anyone else in order to make something of myself. Otherwise, I'm nothing."

His arms encircled her. His face pressed against hers. "Oh, no you're not, little angel."

"You don't know anything."

"I've known some real nothings. And I know you're anything but that."

One of his hands was around her shoulders, the other was tight around her back. Steven was kissing her. KC was kissing him. Hard, furious kisses mixed with tears and wet grass. KC didn't know who had started kissing first. She didn't know what had happened, or when, or how. She couldn't think anymore. All she knew was that her life was a mess. But she didn't care about any of that, because she was kissing Steven Garth.

Here's a sneak preview of
Freshman Guys, *the third*
book in the compelling story
of **FRESHMAN DORM.**

*W*elcome everyone. Welcome to our Tri Beta homecoming." Courtney Conner stood at the head of the reception line wearing a black velvet smock with a lace collar.

Lauren froze, waiting for Courtney to notice Dash.

With perfect poise, Courtney put out her hand in greeting. She looked right at Dash but didn't react. "Hello."

"Hi." Lauren nervously pushed her glasses against her nose. She turned to Dash and almost stepped on his foot. "This is Dash Ramirez."

"Have we met?" Courtney asked him, all polite innocence.

Dash smiled as if he saw right through her. "Somehow I don't think we travel in the same circles."

"Dash is an assistant editor of *The U of S Weekly Journal*," Lauren explained.

"Well, I'm very glad to meet you Mr. Ramirez," responded Courtney, smooth as honey. "Welcome to our open house. Isn't it exciting that we won the game?"

Dash nodded.

"I don't suppose you're going to do an article on us? What would you write about?"

"Who knows?" Dash rocked on his high tops and began taking in the scene. "Anything's possible."

Lauren finally noticed a flicker of alarm in Courtney's eyes.

"Well do look around. I'm president of this sisterhood. If you need any information, you can always ask me." Courtney smiled and turned to the next guest.

"That Courtney is slick," Dash muttered as they made their way away from the line. He wrung out his hand. "I haven't done that much greeting since my cousin Enrique's wedding."

That was when Lauren spotted Marielle Danner and a few of the more boot-licking pledges coming toward them like a hungry wolf pack.

Marielle stopped, and the pledges fell in behind her. She surveyed Lauren's outfit. "Lauren," Marielle cooed, her hair swishing as she tossed her head. "I thought we talked about these new clothes of yours." She waved a finger and her charm bracelet clanked. "You look . . . interesting."

The other pledges tee-heed.

Marielle then honed in on Dash. "Who do we have here?"

"I'm Dash Ramirez," he said.

"Dash?" Marielle scoffed. "Is that a nickname?"

"Short for Dashiell. Like Dashiell Hammet. He was a writer. Even hear of him?"

Marielle looked blank.

Dash didn't back down. "And who are you?"

"Dash, this is Marielle Danner," Lauren said.

"So who are you, though?" Marielle insisted. "I mean, why should I care about who you are?"

Dash stiffened and Lauren knew he was ready to walk away.

"Dash is on the staff of *The Weekly Journal*," Lauren stammered.

"Do you write stories, like Lauren does?"

Dash narrowed his dark eyes. "I'm a journalist."

Marielle kept sneering down her turned up nose. "How do you get ideas for your articles?"

"I steal them," Dash told her, his face relaxing in an ironic smile.

"When do you write?"

"Late at night under a full moon."

The pledges giggled. Now Lauren smiled as well.

"Do you write by hand or on a word processor?"

"I prefer to write in blood." Dash swaggered. "But when that's not available I use a 1947 Royal typewriter that weighs about forty seven hundred pounds and takes six people to push down the keys."

Now the pledges started firing questions, too, with Marielle watching, her pretty face contorted in a frown.

"Is there anything you won't write about, Dash?"

"Boring stuff. Television. Yacht races. What goes on in places like this."

"This isn't boring."

"True, it's not as boring as a story on kitchen appliances or lawn fertilizers. Or"—Dash looked over at the buffet table—"hors d'oeuvres."

To Lauren's amazement, the pledges laughed again. A couple of active members noticed the huddle and joined in.

"Okay," another pledge insisted, "what would you write if you were going to write about the Tri Beta house though? I mean honestly."

Dash looked at Lauren and rolled his eyes. "Well, first of all I hardly every write 'honestly.' I prefer to write 'frankly,' but sometimes I'll just settle for 'truthfully.' Second, it seems to me I was asked that question when I came in. Any of you believe in déjà voodoo?"

"Déjà what?"

Lauren spun around to locate the new, smooth, dusky voice. Courtney had joined the group and was staring at Dash, too. Lauren wondered if Marielle had called Courtney over, if every word of Dash's were being recorded as evidence for Lauren's expulsion in a sorority supreme court. She hoped so.

The pledges sensed Courtney's disapproval of Dash, and began to back away, whispering among themselves. A few turned for one last look at Dash, but soon they had all rejoined the rest of the homecoming Tri Beta crowd.

Lauren and Dash were alone again.

Lauren exhaled. She hadn't realized how tense she was. Her fists were clenched and her neck ached. "Can we get some air? I think that's about all I can take for a while."

"Me, too," he whispered. "I've got to make some posters for tomorrow's protest. Some other time."

Lauren wasn't sure who was in a bigger hurry to leave as they scooted together out the front door.

As soon as the Tri Beta house was behind them, Dash began whistling *Who's Afraid of the Big Bad Wolf*. Soon Lauren joined in and then they were skipping and laughing. Lauren was even leaping and tapping at leaves hanging from trees. For once in her life, she felt light, giddy, even triumphant. When they passed the Kappa house, Dash nodded at two sorority sisters.

"Fappa, Epsilon, Hamma," he said solemnly and nodded.

The girls glared at him and walked faster.

"I wish I could hear what the Tri Betas are saying about me now," Lauren said. She stopped and put her face in her hands. "No, I don't," she admitted. "I really don't want to know."

They stood on the sidewalk watching a frat pack walk by. Finally Lauren spoke up again. "Do you live in the dorms?"

"I live off campus. I can walk."

"You sure you don't want a ride?"

"Nah. It's not far."

Lauren lingered. "Thanks for coming with me to this."

"Hey, don't thank me. You were the one taking a chance, letting a heathen like me in a place like that. It took some guts."

"Not really."

"Oh, yeah." He stuck his hands in his pockets and looked at the ground. "From what I've heard they tie you up and make you chant secret sorority songs just for looking at guys like me."

Looking at him? Lauren felt breathless. Had she been *looking* at him? Was it at all possible that Dash saw her in that way? Since she had next to no experience with guys, she really didn't know.

"Anyway," she said. "I don't care what they do. I want to quit soon anyway."

"Yeah?" Lightly, almost imperceptibly, he reached over and touched her shoulder. His dark eyes became softer, almost fuzzy. "I knew there was something I liked about you."

"Really?"

He shrugged. "Sure."

A little embarrassed, Dash started to walk away. "Okay. Well. See you tomorrow."

"See you then."

He waved. "Tomorrow we make things change."

"Goodbye."

Lauren opened the door to her car and realized that she couldn't wait for things to change. She was suddenly ready for her entire life to be transformed.

Coming in November,
a thrilling new series,
HORROR HIGH. Here's
a preview from Book #1,
Mr. Popularity.

*J*ake watched in his rearview mirror as the 280ZX swung around to pull beside his green Chevy. Brad was driving out of control in the wrong lane. He honked his horn and swerved from side to side, screaming wildly. There was an eerie, glazed expression on his face.

Holding steady to the wheel, Jake glared over at Brad. "Are you crazy, Forester? Stop it!"

The voices were raging inside Brad. They told him to get Jake now, to run him off the cliffs that dropped into Lighthouse Bay. If he didn't stop Jake, Jake would steal Cassie from him.

Jake looked at the cliffs that appeared suddenly on his right. They weren't far from Indian Point. The road began to curve a little. Suddenly a large delivery truck rounded the bend, coming straight toward a head-on collision with Brad's car.

"Forester!" Jake cried.

Brad downshifted, slipping behind the Chevy. The delivery truck shot past them. Brad swung his car into the passing lane again, roaring up next to the Chevy.

"Race me!" Brad cried.

Jake shook his fist at Brad. "Are you crazy?"

"Race me!"

"Forget it, you psycho!"

"Chicken!"

Jake eased off the accelerator, trying to slow down. The road had begun to wind in a series of long curves that followed the angles of the cliffs. Brad went after Jake again, cutting in front of the Chevy. Jake had to slam on the brakes. The Chevy began to spin out of control.

Jake held tightly to the wheel as his car careened toward the cliffs. It was a fifty-foot drop to the waters of Lighthouse Bay.

Brad's car swerved back toward the highway, its tires screeching on the pavement. Jake tried to straighten out the Chevy, but the back wheels started to slip off the edge of the cliffs.

When the Chevy came to a stop, Jake started to open the door, but when he shifted his weight, the car tilted backward. He had to lean forward again to keep from plummeting into the bay.

He saw the red car backing up toward him. When he was about ten feet away, Brad stopped his car and got out. A weird smile spread over Brad's lips. He got back into his car. The red vehicle began to roll slowly toward the dangling Chevy.

"No!" Jake cried.

He tried to open the door again, but the Chevy tilted toward the water below. Jake threw his weight forward. The red car was still coming, inch by inch. Brad intended to ram the Chevy and knock Jake over the cliffs.

The evil voices were congratulating Brad on a job well done. He would be rid of his problem once and for all, clearing the way for him to be with Cassie.

"No!" Jake shouted. "Don't do it, Forester."

Brad moved slowly, making his enemy sweat. He wanted Jake to suffer before he died. The longer it took, the more Brad could savor the victory.

Jake cried out again, pleading for his life. He clung helplessly to the steering wheel. But Brad kept coming.

Brad's eyes were wide. Suddenly he saw a flash of white as it appeared on the highway to his right. The sheriff's patrol car headed straight for them, stopping on the shoulder of the road.

The deputy gawked at the Chevy. "My sweet Lord!

Hold on there, boy! Don't move!" He got out of the patrol car.

Brad had to apply the brakes. Luckily the patrolman was the same deputy he had bribed earlier that morning. Brad straightened himself, ready to go into his Mr. Popularity act. He knew he had to be convincing to pull it off.

Brad stepped out of his car. "I was driving by, officer," he said in a concerned tone. "I saw this guy in trouble."